HALF WAY IN LOVE

HOW FAR WILL YOU GO IN LOVE, WHEN YOU KNOW THAT YOU CANT HAVE IT

VIJAY NAIR

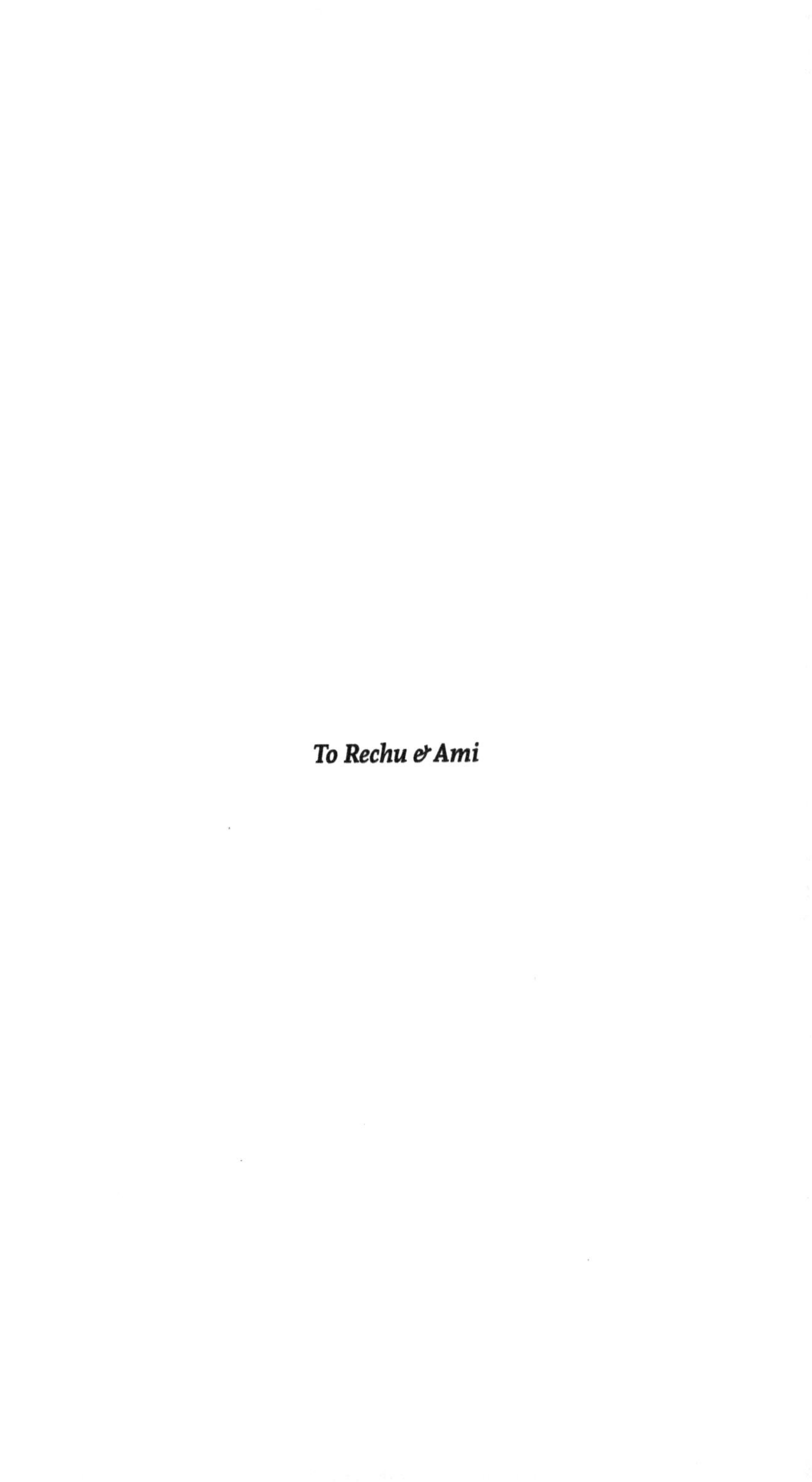

To Rechu & Ami

Contents

Contents

Foreword

"Halfway in Love"- is a romantic novel from the pen of a Cotton mill employee- turned Naval person-turned Banker-turned Author. Mr. Vijay Nair with his rich life experience and acute observation skill, has created a beautiful world within his debut Novel.

Even though I do not read romance genre, I took this book for reading as Vijay is a fellow Banker and part of our Talented Bankers' community. Also, as contemporary English writers from Kerala are rare, and that too from banking fraternity, I strongly felt that those who write deserve support.

Though I write (stories) both in English and Malayalam, I generally feel that I can express more impactfully in English. But to bring out the finest of emotions, one best needs to resort to mother tongue. This, we can see in this novel too. The Author has included verses in Malayalam to convey protagonist's feelings towards his love. I do not know if that had ever happened in an Indian English Novel.

The ease of reading got me hooked into the book and prompted me to finish it at one-go. It's a simple, straightforward, honest narration. Ofcourse, the story has its elements of surprises too.

Story depicts the world of Dev- Devanarayan, who grows in life initially with the support of a girl and then by his own hardwork and passion. It's a slap from authority - rather an insult, that turns his life 360 degree. It's not purely a rag-to-riches story. Dev could have continued to live as an ordinary person. But the presence of Sukanya, and her influence, fuels his growth. She gives the much needed push which kickstarts the rise in stature of Dev.

Dev becomes a multimillionaire. This alone should be inspiring for any reader. Yet the story doesn't end there. Instead it begins from there.

In due course of his business, while leading a mundane life, he meets his sweetheart Revathy, who is a Banker. Rest of the story is told with the thoughts, emotions and actions of the protoganist and the lovely times he spends with Revathy.

What happens to their romance? whether the romance actually bloomed ?

or was it one-sided? why and how is the climax of the novel? Questions keep piling up as you go on turning the pages. but when it ends, one can't get over the feeling of need for more. That, the end of the story is not the definite end. That, It's just a semicolon. The Author definitely leaves space for a captivating sequel.

There are many types of contemporary romance novels- General contemporary romance, Romantic suspense, Baby love,

Medical romance, Cowboy contemporary romance, Glamour and jet set, Humorous contemporary romance, International lovers, Long Distance Relationships and so on.

"Halfway in Love"- to me is an "Inspiring and Tragic Romance".

The writer is careful about the scenes and sentences. The values he upholds is clearly visible in the narrations. There's a very thin line between Romance and Erotica. But I can vouch that this is a clean desi love story. "It's for the young adults too", the writer had told me.

Another interesting element in the novel is the description of Isha Foundation, the ashram and Adiyogi statue, situated at coimbatore. Being a keen follower of spiritual teachings of Sadguru, I thoroughly enjoyed the chapter in which the protagonists visit the Isha Foundation. What a divine atmosphere!

Having read all of Chetan Bhagat's books, I could see glimpses of his brilliance in many places in this novel. It's a happy thing that we Keralites finally have our own "Chetan Bhagat" - Vijay Nair.

The most amazing thing about the novel is that the author wrote this in just 23 days. We must expect so much more from this budding writer. In a book market where the selling theme is dominated with "heavy" plots like mystery, thriller, crime, investigation, suspense etc., a light novel like this gives you a pleasant and positive feeling, longing for more to read.

I am wishing Vijay Nair all the very best and waiting to read more from his pen.

Sandhya Naren

(Sandhya Naren is a banker and a Finance columnist at SheSight International Women's Magazine. She has published her stories in various Anthologies. She also tells stories in English and multiple Indian languages under her venture "Kathamadhuram". She is Co-founder of "Manasa Learning Solutions"- Personal Finance training academy for women and children.)

Preface

Dear readers,

Very happy to join you all again with the third edition of my debut novel, Half way in Love.

It has been a humbling journey since the release of my debut novel. People have been pouring in their good words personally over phone and social media and also have been magnanimous in global reviews. I am touched beyond words.

For those who expressed their concerns about Dev and Revathy, those with the most beautiful of hearts, there is a sequel coming. It is not the end of the world for them. Request all to wait till then, for a magical ending to their wonderful love story.

And for my new readers, who have just stepped in, you are invited to the charismatic world of Dev. Story of a young man, who start as a labourer boy in the hosiery town of Tirupur and go on to become one of the top builders of Kerala. He is not alone here. Revathy steps in with her grace and beauty.

So, before I reveal too much here, welcome to the world of Dev and Revathy.

With love,
Vijay Nair

Acknowledgements

Thank you,

God, for giving me this wonderful opportunity called life.

Mom & Dad, for bringing me up with wisdom, compassion and love.

My teachers, on and off the campus, academic and non-academic, who taught me how to handle this life.

My class mates from Jawahar Navodaya Vidyalaya, who keep investing their trust on me and make me believe I am super good.

My colleagues at SBI, who keep encouraging me.

Anagha Vinod, my niece, who designed beautiful cover pages for the first edition of my book.

And you readers; for actually selecting this book from among the many that pop up in search window, picking up from the book shelves and for investing your valuable time in reading this book.

ONE

I was keenly observing the young man sitting opposite to me, uncomfortably spread out on the Italian Sofa.

He seemed overwhelmed with emotions.

He was handsome, tall and was a true specimen of the upper class society.

Except the unshaven chin.

Just above 26 years of age.

Dev. Devanarayan.

He was looking vacantly at the tiny elephant figures, which were fine display of Mahabalipuram craftsmanship, placed on the teapoy.

He was holding a cup of coffee with both hands, which Gayathri had given him minutes before. He was feeling its warmth on his palms.

For me, I had just finished an interview, with a celebrated youtuber.

It was the fourth interview of the day for me.

I was clearly drained out and weary.

Two novels, in last 3 years. Both went on to become best sellers. The second one was now being scripted into a film.

Third book was already announced by my publisher.

Two chapters more, to complete the book. Two chapters more, to relieve me of the pain of creation, which I have been going through, for past 9 months.

Laptop was still open on the teapoy, into which I was furiously typing in, as the plot kept unwinding thick and fast in my mind.

Until this guy intervened.

A gentle push at the calling bell, and that brisk and lost walk to my sofa.

He said nothing.

He still sat there, as if in a confusion how to start.

And I was too moved, to disturb his silence.

Till I could stand no more.

"Dev..."

I had only started when he raised his head to look into my face.

His eyes were wet. And a faint smile appeared on his face.

"She survived..."

He said, rubbing his tears with left hand.

Gayathri walked in quickly to take back the tea cup. She must have been listening to Dev's words. I could see tears in her eyes too. She turned back towards the kitchen, very quick, may be in an attempt to hide her emotions

Deep silence. I kept looking at him. I was too happy to speak anything.

Slowly, I stood up, and walked to him, and embraced him in a soft hug.

"Thank god Dev. His blessings are with you."

My eyes turned quickly to the monitor of the laptop, to the last lines of the chapter I was typing in;

"Dev stooped over Revathy. He watched her bleed through her stomach, pierced by a sharp knife...

her wonderful eyes fixed on him,

.. lifeless."

I patted his shoulder, to comfort him, and walked out of his hug to take my seat beside the laptop.

And deleted the last word.

I could hear Gayathri breaking out in kitchen.

TWO

Few months back.

"I think I am going to write about him, Gachu. Dev's story will be my third book".

I was speaking to Gayathri, my eyes fixed on the newspaper. I could hear her working in open kitchen. I had just returned back from dropping my kid to school.

It's a huge relief. A relief that you get after you finally drop your kid to school. After all those tiring morning tantrums.

Making her do home works at last minute, rehearsing her speech for the morning assembly, ironing her uniforms, polishing the shoes, making her eat, getting her ready, speeding her to school in car, praying hard that goddamn railway gate won't close for at least today.

It was when I reached out to the tea cup,that I realized there was no response from Gayathri until now.

I looked at her.

What now?

She was looking at me, hands folded, her cheeks flared up.

Though obviously angry for some reason, she looked cute.

"What happened? Why are you staring at me like that?"

"And, Gachu, for god's sake, turn off the gas. Milk is about to over flow".

I learnt not to take on a wife while cooking.

Milk overflowed.

I rushed to turn off the gas.

"What Gachu, what happened now?"

"You said, third book will be about us"

She drew on, seriously hurt.

"I have even told my friends, that this time it will be us. They are too curious to read our story . And mind you, they are your huge fans.

Reshma's face suddenly appeared in high definition image. I deleted it in haste.

I went near her, placed my hands on her hips and drew her close, to a hug.

"I am reserving my best to it sweet heart. Next one, I promise. This time let it be Dev. Devanarayan."

"Dev?"

"Yeah, I told you no, the guy who gave me a lift last night. It has been only a day of knowing him, and he is seriously making me to focus my thoughts on him"

"Is he that interesting, this Dev?"

"Yes Gachu. He is interesting. "

A lightning struck somewhere nearby, followed by a loud thunder. Gayathri shook a bit. She stuck to me more closely.

"And, his story is more interesting"

I could feel Gayathri's head on my shoulder.

I knew, I got my approval.

THREE

A night, few months back...

"What is it Arjun?"

He had braked the car suddenly, and the car turned and stopped safely, just clear of the road.

"Tyre burst sir. Front right".

Arjun is a responsible driver. His gift is that he reads my mind. When I am in a hurry, he drives fast. When I require peace, or prepare presentations on the way, he drives it steadily. Almost of my age, he has been my reliable guy for past five years.

We were coming back from a felicitation ceremony organised by a renowned college in Coimbatore. A new role, I was being dragged into. A motivational speaker.

Writers and motivations!

It was past eleven at night. We had reached Navakkarai, and were stranded just in front of Nandi temple. The temple had a huge statue of Nandi. I have heard many illegimate stories about how Nandi statue is growing in size every day.

Arjun was punching the tyre to ascertain its condition.

"What the f... Arjun, even this One crore car?"

He smiled at me faintly.

"Temperature fluctuations sir, may be."

I smiled back realising the foolishness of my words. I had tripped off into a half sleep during the drive back. I opened my eyes only when the car shook hard with the sudden brake.

"What do we do now?"

My thoughts went flying home to Gayathri and kid. She had called twenty minutes before, and I had assured her that I will be home in next forty minutes.

"It is doubtful, whether we can get a tyre guy now. I will get you a lift sir, and you go home please. Not the right place, at this time sir. All those fake accidents and deaths that we keep hearing about. Not at all right."

I understood the gravity of his words. I too had heard many stories of accidents and sabotages of luxury and semi luxury cars in recent times.

"What you will do, Arjun?"

"Don't worry sir. I have a friend nearby. I will stay in his home. You go home peacefully".

And thus we waited, near the edge of the road. For a lift.

Vehicles were whizzing past, mercilessly.

It is only when you stand out on the road and watch the vehicles passing by, you realise the actual speed at which they pass. With a chill in spine.

We were in the receding phase of the second wave of Covid 19. The chances of getting a lift, was less.

Still, we waited, for that person, who will rise above all apprehensions and lend a helping hand to the people stranded on the road.

God always has his plans for us. Even while we are sleeping tight on our beds;

or are helplessly stranded out on the road at midnight.

It must have been a Toyota Fortuner, as I could make out from the shape of headlamps from a distance.

We waved our hands, in hope.

And, this time the vehicle slowed down, and came to a halt near us.

After a second of observing us, may be, the left window glass came sliding down.

"Bharath Sir? What happened?"

The person in the driving seat asked.

I felt touched. Someone recognised me, at this hour, at this remote place.

Before I could answer, Arjun, desperate to get me home, intervened, keeping his head down to look at the driver and answered.

"Tyre burst sir",

"can you please drop him to the nearest place where he can catch an auto ?"

He asked. Then, with a shock, as he recognised the person at the wheel.

"Sir, you are..,"

Arjun, scratched his head as if to retrieve the name of the face he had recongnised at once.

The face felt familiar to me too. But I was too touched by this guy stopping, and recognising me, his familiarity by passed my brain. It was clogged already with some sort of happiness.

It doesn't take much to be happy.

"I am Dev, Devanarayan". He answered Arjun.

Arjun, stood, stranded on the road, his mouth wide open in some sort of shock, as we sped away from him.

Now I turned slowly towards him.

A handsome, clean shaven man, in his mid twenties.

"Dev Narayan, of the Emerald Builders? and the Emerald Mall? A real honour."

I said, without making any attempt to hide my surprise.

"Just Dev, Devanarayan, sir. Your huge fan. Read both your books. Something in those words of yours. Truely inspired. I never thought I would pick up the very own Bharath on my way back from Coimbatore."

He laughed affably.

I thanked his words in a smile.

"Can you WhatsApp me the location of your home sir?" He asked, after a pause.

I did.

He copied it to his navigation system and drove now in silence.

"Where did you go? I didn't know the super-rich like you drove around on your own." I asked.

I could see his face suddenly turning red, and his lips joining in a shy smile.

"I went to airport to drop someone."

That shy smile still remained on his face. He was not aware that I was noticing.

"Your girlfriend?"

Driving alone, at this hour, one of the top builders of Kerala...

You don't require the services of celebrated Mr. Sherlock Holmes for that deduction.

He turned to face me now.

"She is Revathy. I don't know whether you can call her my girlfriend."

"Not yet"

He completed after a pause.

His smile, betrayed his words.

And next forty minutes, I listened to his story.

FOUR

Some months back.

"Chief minister will be here anytime now"

Joy, the firebrand MLA, and a long time friend, whispered sitting next to Dev.

He smiled in reply. Though he could feel adrenalin pumping up on the entire dais, Dev was abnormally calm.

A calmness, which engulfs a battle field, after the last drop of blood has been shed, after the last breath has been taken, after the battle has been won.

Calmness of a warrior who wins the deciding battle.

The cuts and bruises didn't ache any more.

He knew he had grown in cult, larger enough to rope in the Chief Minister himself for inaugurating his Shopping mall. The biggest in Palakkad. And infact the second largest in whole Kerala.

The Emerald Mall.

A pet project, of the Emerald Builders, found by him.

Total retail space of 19,00,000 sq ft and 250 plus stores. And a hypermarket. It had one of the largest indoor entertainment zones in the country, multilevel car parking space for more than 3,000 cars and a food court with a capacity for 2000 people serving various regional, international and specialty cuisines. To top it all, it boasted of an 8 screen Multiplex including 4DX screen. Huge indeed.

It was inside Emerald Project, a luxurious villas project spread over hundred acres of prime land, bordering NH 544.

Even Dev never expected it to be so huge.

But the success of luxury villa projects, gave him the necessary funding for going this big.

Every Emerald project has been a grand success since their launches. This one bordering the NH was ninth of them.

Almost all of the luxury villas in this particular project, One hundred fifty of them, sold like hot cakes. He himself lived in one of the largest one. Sprawling over two acres of land.

Villa No. 45.

Now, the mall, to be inaugurated today.

It was jam packed already.

District police had a hard time controlling the crowd and the heavy traffic volumes. Their headache increased, as the chief minister was attending the function along with two other ministers.

Dev thanked Joy, the third time MLA, in mind. Without him, all these arrangements could never have been made.

He was the one who was instrumental in getting the Chief Minister's date and all the police support.

There was heavy media presence since eight in the morning.

Now it was almost nearing eleven.

It is time. Dev muttered to himself.

And CM's barricade arrived in usual pomp and splendour.

The band, started playing, as Chief Minister got out from his Toyota Crysta.

The crowd erupted into cheers and applause on seeing his face.

He waved at everyone, and walked among tight security to the dais.

Dais was set up in the central hall, with all the floors having a view of the dais. All floors were jam packed.

Chief Minister reached the dais. All stood up in respect. He wished every one with a namaste, and a wonderful smile. He reached Dev.

His smile broadened in appreciation.

"You are too young to be building this, Dev. Amazing hard work. My best wishes".

Dev's eyes now got moist.

He uttered a thanks with folded hands and a grateful smile.

The inaugural function started.

With prayer.

The event management company was spot on. Their anchors, ushers, program managers and everything else. Everything was so perfect.

The anchor announced the Chief Minister to formally inaugurate the Mall now.

He got up and walked to the mic with steady steps. He adjusted the mic and started.

There was pin drop silence now in the crowd.

"Good morning all, and a big namaste".

He then continued with formal acknowledgements of the dignitaries sitting on the dais. Each in turn returned their gesture standing up and folding their hands in a namaste.

"And coming to the founder of this Mall."

Everyone got silent once again. Dev sat tight in his chair. He was overcome with emotions.

"You all know Dev, Devanarayan. He is a familiar face now. I am proud of him as he is too young to be building a mall of this size. I appreciate his hard work and dedication."

Dev, tears in eyes, folded his hands in acknowledgement.

"But, what I want all to know is, how he reached the position that he is in now"

Dev now looked at CM in disbelief. How could he know?

He looked at Joy. He smiled in affirmation.

Dev understood why he is CM after all.

He does his homework. And he had taken pain to know about him, research on him, before coming here.

Dev now looked earnestly at CM, for taking in his words. How much did he know??

CM continued in a sober voice now.

"It all started with a tight slap. When he was just twenty"

He continued, in detail, how Dev became Devanarayan of today.

And the crowd sat in utter disbelief. Listening to his words, with their eyes fixed on Devanarayan.

Dev sat, physically rooted to his chair. But his soul travelled back in time, to that dingy office room, of a knitting company, somewhere in Tirupur, Tamilnadu.

He stood there, in front of ruffian of a boss, rubbing his cheeks.

"...and I have the honour to formally inaugurate the Emerald Mall."

CM was concluding now.

"Congratulations Palakkad, and thank you Dev, for being what you are and doing what you can, for this state and the country. Thank you all.

Crowd erupted again.

Dev mechanically followed the CM, to the battery cart, with other ministers and Joy and rode forward to have a round of the mall.

But his thoughts rode back, at lightning speed, to that dingy office.

FIVE

It was a small, dingy, dimly lit office room.

It looked like an office room only because of the presence of a table and chair.

Walls were not plastered or painted.

It had asbestos sheets as roof. A ceiling fan rotated above, which declined to pick up speed even when put on its top speed mode.

On the table, lay a half open English Daily.

It was the office of the proprietor of a knitting company in Tirupur.

The Sakthi Mills.

Named after its proprietor.

Adjacent to the office, around ten knitting machines ran round the clock with heavy sound, turning cotton yarns into cotton cloth rolls.

Sakthi had walked into office after lunch break, when his manager Ramakrishnan broke this news to him.

He had caught Dev, the new recruit, reading English newspaper which was meant for the boss.

And that too sitting in his office.

A tight slap followed.

A twenty year old Dev, stood before this bull dog, rubbing his cheek.

"That slap is for two things you stupid. One, you were reading newspaper when you were supposed to break your back in that gutter..."

He roared, pointing his left thumb towards the knitting floor, where the machines kept grumbling.

"And you were reading my newspaper sitting in my office. You young filths think yourself smart after few years in school."

Another slap.

Dev lost his balance, and managed not to fall on the floor.

Shocked and humiliated, he was unable to speak anything.

He was just one week into this company. In fact, his father had got him this position. His father worked as a night watchman, in Pin Knitting company, run by Sakthi's elder brother, Ramalingam. Ramalingam liked Dev's father, Sundaram. So when Sundaram went with an appeal to get his son a job, Ramalingam called his younger brother to take in Dev.

"Remember, take care of Dev. He is Sundaram's son. None of your rash ways with him".

Ramalingam had added, knowing very well what his younger brother was like.

Dropped out of college after being rusticated by college authorities for his misdeeds, Sakthi was always a head ache to the well-known business family of Tirupur. They went back generations in hosiery business.

Unlike his elder brothers, Sakthi was an immense alcoholic. And when on poison, he was a devil.

But Sakthi was particularly careful with Dev. Ramu brother's order. He never dared to touch the boy. Until this afternoon. Until he was brainwashed by Ramakrishnan.

One week had gone peacefully. Dev was learning things quick. But, Ramakrishnan, the floor manager was not happy with the way Dev was meted out preferential treatment.

He had reasons to hate the boy, from the very second day of Dev in the company.

Ramky, as he was called, and Sakthi had a habit of having a drink in the office every afternoon.

On the second day of Dev's arrival in the company, Ramky took out the unwashed glasses from previous day's drinks session. He called out to Dev.

"Dev, wash these glasses and bring"

Dev, hurried towards office from the machine floor.

Sakthi, who was glancing over the newspaper, turned to Ramky and admonished him with his eyes.

Ramky was hurt. He got the message.

He turned off Dev, and walked to the sink to wash the glasses himself, every cells in his body burning.

This boy should not be pampered like this forever. He wanted someone under him to do all dirty works. He didn't want someone who needs to be pampered.

Need to do something. And he waited for a chance.

And today he got one.

Sakthi had probably hopped into Le Pebble bar, and had his quota of drinks, on the way back from his lunch. It was his practice on some days.

And he was devil himself today.

He turned to the boy and shouted.

"Get lost, before I kick you next"

"Enough of this shit". Dev told himself.

Ignoring Sakthi's order, he walked towards the main door.

"Where are you going bastard? I said go and rot among the machines".

Sakthi shouted, like a man possessed.

Dev, now having taken his decision in mind, stopped and turned to face him.

"Not any more sir. I am going home. You can record my resignation. "

Dev, turned and pulled open the office main door.

There, a young girl was standing. Listening to all that was happening inside. Looking at him now, with concern.

He recognised her, from some photographs he had seen on Sakthi's table.

Sukanya.

Daughter of Sakthi.

He looked at her passively, and walked out, with multiple injuries to his heart.

Into the scorching heat. Into the gutter flowing streets.

SIX

"I am sorry dad, I can't continue there".

Dev, narrated his dad the whole story leaving out the slaps he got. He didn't want to make his father sad, by telling him about the slaps.

Sundaram listened to everything silently. He possibly just got up from his sleep, to get ready in time for the night duty.

"Never mind Dev. Leave it. You need not go there. After all those insults". He got up and patted Dev's shoulder.

And his hands moved to Dev's cheeks, in concern.

"Did it hurt?"

His eyes were moist. And he walked away to the common bathroom.

Dev stood shocked. He looked in the direction of kitchen. Sarada, his mother was wiping away her tears with palloo of her sari.

"How you people knew about it mom?" He asked her.

"Sukanya came here Dev. She left just few minutes before. She is very fond of your dad, Dev. He only used to take her to school. She came on her scooty. She told us everything that had happened."

Sarada, continued now in jittery voice.

"Don't go to that damn place dear. I have not brought you up for getting hit by that scoundrel. We share whatever half bread your father brings. That is enough. At least, for the time being."

He now hugged his mom tightly.

"You need not worry mom. I will do something. I don't know what, but I will definitely do something. "

He said, turning his face away from her and letting himself loose from her hug.

Dev sat on the makeshift cot. Sarada came to sit with him.

She lifted his face and looked into his eyes.

She was proud of her son. Tall, handsome, and hints of a fine moustache above the upper lips.

He was the talk among the neighbouring girls ever since he landed from Kerala. Fair skin got instant approval among the locals. And Dev, went after his mom. He was very fair.

He looked out of place in Tirupur with his dashing good looks.

" Sukanya came here for something else Dev. She is a real princess. After her mom. She didn't like the way Sakthi treated you. She said, she wants to help you. "

"She wants to help me? How old is she? fifteen?"

Dev couldn't hide his surprise.

"She is almost your age Dev. Got into first year Engineering. She eats very less. May be that is why she still looks like a small girl."

Sarada continued, thrusting a piece of paper into his hand.

"She told me to give you this."

With that, she took one long look at her son and withdrew herself to kitchen. Sambar, in preparation, was already giving out inviting smell from the kitchen.

He opened the paper.

"Hi... Be there at the entrance of Old bus stand tomorrow at sharp eleven in the morning. Come at any cost. I am bunking class just for this. And this is important.

See you Dev.

Sukanya"

Dev now looked up from the piece of paper.

"I am not going anywhere". Dev shouted out to his mom in kitchen. He secretly wanted his mother's opinion on meeting Sukanya.

Sarada couldn't hide her smile.

"You can go. My son will be safe with her. She wants to take you somewhere. Go wearing that new dress you occasionally wear."

Dev was not sure even now.

Still, he decided he will go. There was something in the tone of her message.

Next day, at ten in the morning, he took the bus from Weavers colony bus stop to Old bus stand. Hits of SP Balasubramaniam and Ilayaraja, the maestro musician of Kollywood, played loudly through speakers. Speakers which seemed to exist all over the bus!

Tamils love everything loud.

Forty five minutes past ten, Dev positioned himself studiously at the entrance of the Old bus stand.

He looked handsome, in his regulation blue jeans and white shirt. A group of girls standing few meters away from him were pointing at him and giggling rather too loudly and unnecessarily. They were being artificially articulate.

Dev stood silently and waited with patience.

11.00 AM.

A scooty slid from behind and stopped near him sleekly.

Sukanya.

His head turned and he felt weak in stomach.

She was wearing sunglasses. Clad in a jeans and a t shirt with quotes, she looked very pretty and neat.

"Hi Dev, get on the scooty."

She said and indicated to the vacant pillion space.

"Never mind the girls", she added, as she saw the group of girls now eyeing them with suspicion.

"You will have tough time living in Tirupur, Mr. Aravind Samy"

She giggled.

Aravind Samy, a leading Tamil actor, was the comparison tamils used for any fair and handsome guy. He was their reference value.

Dev sneaked on the pillion space, at a safe distance behind Sukanya. She was off in a second towards the busy main road.

"You will fall down Dev. You can hold on to me".

Sukanya shouted to him, without looking back. Somehow, she looked happy.

Dev's hands were trembling now.

He now placed his trembling hands, on her shoulder. It felt like rose petals.

He felt a slight shiver, from her body, on his first touch.

She made it up with a sudden increase in throttle.

Dev was sweating now.

He prayed she would soon reach, where ever she was taking him now.

And next two minutes, scooty stopped in the parking space of the State Bank.

Dev, now reluctant to let go of the rose petals, sat still for fraction of a second.

"Get down hero. We need to make it quick. Can't hang around with you for ever."

She laughed beautifully.

Dev slid out, with a shy smile.

"Thank god, you smiled. Come now. We are going to see the Branch Manager."

And she started walking beautifully towards the entrance.

With mixed emotions, Dev followed her, into the banking hall.

SEVEN

It was the commercial branch of the State Bank.

"Are you ok? Where are you taking me?"

Dev kept his voice low. He was first time into a bank. The glass cabins, formally dressed employees and crowded banking hall gave him some kind of nervousness.

She turned to him and rolled her eyes in a sweet, admonishing way, keeping one hand on her hips. He understood what it meant.

He shut up.

She walked straight to Branch Manager's cabin.

Dev could see a man in early fifties, sweating even in the air-conditioned room, and typing furiously at the key board.

She looked into the cabin through the half glass door, and waved at him.

"What is she into..? " Dev wondered. But he didn't dare to ask her.

On seeing her, the Manager got up from his table with a smile, and pulled open the door for them.

"Hi, uncle. Hope you are not busy. Troubling you anyway. Hope Lakshmi told you I was coming."

She went on at a speed, most of the sports cars would fail.

" Yes, she told me. Come sit Sukanya. And you too Dev."

Dev looked at him with a how do you know question in his eyes.

"I know you Dev. Lakshmi had told me about you."

"But not wise to bunk your classes."

He continued turning to Sukanya now.

"You could have come after your college too".

Probably her classmate's father. Dev looked at his name board on the table.

Ananthanarayanan, Chief Manager.

He seemed a reasonable guy altogether.

Sakthi's face flashed in his mind for a second. Two extremes of human race. He got that burning sensation again.

Now, assuming the business like posture, Chief Manager asked Sukanya.

"So you are saying he wants to start a business. And you want me to finance his business. Is that right dear?"

" Yes uncle"

Dev now looked at her with disbelief. What is going on. Business, me? When did I tell her?

Over the corner of her eyes, Sukanya watched him asking questions to her. She stopped him once again with that trademark rolling of her eyes.

Dev kept quiet again.

"What business is he going to do? Or rather, you want him to do?"

He again asked, with a smile.

Experience does make one wise. He did all the talking to Sukanya. He knew she was taking the lead.

Dev prayed god, the manager won't ask him anything.

"Uncle, he will do sub works for hosiery export companies. I have talked to few guys there. They are ready to help him. Please uncle, you provide him the loan, to start off with. Like, the stitching machines, the tables, chairs for employees, and you know what all. "

She was indeed an heir to the business family she belonged to. Dev, kept looking at her, as she kept on talking to the manager, with loving animations of her hands.

Dev, noticed now, she was beautiful.

And when she was over with the Manager, she had left him no choice. He could not doubt her business acumen. It ran in the family.

All the family business, of Sukanya, operated their banking transactions through this branch. She was a known face, even before Lakshmi became her class mate.

He gave her a checklist, a list of documents required, for sanctioning of the loan.

"Minimum documents required dear".

He answered her 'now what uncle?' look.

"We have to satisfy the auditors. The business part, I will take the risk. It is on me. Don't worry about it Sukanya dear. Dev will start his own company. But guide him. Without you, he will be lost."

She looked at Dev sweetly, pampering him with her eyes.

Dev felt shy. He couldn't meet her eyes and tuned his face slightly away. She was smiling.

She picked up the checklist from the table and pinged Dev to get up.

" Thank you sir". Dev folded his arms in namaste. And smiled at him in gratitude.

He just wanted to thank him. Though, he half understood the whole drama.

Here is a man who is willing to help him. He understood that part.

" Thank you uncle, and see you again with documents. "

Sukanya smiled at him, and walked to the door.

Dev followed her.

"I am hungry", she said, walking towards the nearby bakery.

They sat opposite each other with a cup of tea.

"You want something else?"

She asked while munching her cheese buns. Dev said no.

He continued looking at her, with amusement. Sukanya saw him eyeing her even while she kept sipping her tea. A faint smile appeared on her face.

Girls have two eyes and multiple visions!!

"Why are you doing all this for me, Sukanya. Does your father know?"

"Don't care much about that Dev. You finish your tea. Have to call too many people to get your things done."

"And go home safely," She continued with a mischievous tone;

"don't get groped by local girls on your way home."

She laughed, covering her mouth. She looked cute.

And she started her scooty.

"You know Dev, why I am concerned about you?"

She asked in a low voice now.

Her eyes were moist.

"I didn't like what my father did to you yesterday. In fact I don't like many things that he does. I felt sorry for you."

"And one more thing Dev. I love your father. Probably, I like him more than my dad. He was my Mr. Dependable ever since I was a kid. He took care of me, he dropped me school every day, brought my meals, took care of my needs. I don't want him to get hurt."

"And.." she drew on..

"From what I heard about you from your father, you are not bad too."

She rubbed her eyeliner done eyes.

"And go home Young Turk. We have works to do starting tomorrow. And find a name for your company."

She giggled.

One last look at him, and she slid away.

Dev, kept looking at her receding figure, till she turned a corner and was gone.

He walked towards the bus stand to catch a bus back. Only now he realised how hot the sun was.

"I should not disappoint this girl. For all that she is doing for me, I must not disappoint her."

And he had made up his mind by the time he reached his bus stop. Challenge accepted, @ Sukanya.

EIGHT

It all takes is, a gentle push from someone. To change your thinking, to come out of your mould, to do what you thought you were incapable of doing.

Sukanya did that exactly to Dev.

She guided Dev, into a new channel. She made him to think, which was unthinkable for him, a few days ago.

Dev, quickly unlearned the labourer mindset.

Now, he devoted all his time, towards getting his factory up and running.

It was 2015.

PM Mudra Yojana was launched by Prime Minister of India.

For providing unsecured loans up to ten lakh rupees to the non-corporate, non-farm small/micro enterprises.

It was a huge step, by the Government of India.

It gave the necessary funding and direction to many youths and entrepreneurs.

Funding was the main issue for many aspiring entrepreneurs. Who had the right idea and zeal but lacked funds.

PM mudra Yojana filled the gap.

Dev was one of the initial beneficiaries. And Sukanya made it possible.

How does she know so much? At her age, Dev understood, she was too well informed.

Business ran in her blood.

Manager had given them a half page check list, for sanctioning the loan.

Sukanya seemed to have tie ups with almost half the people of Tirupur.

Everything was done with comparative ease.

Sukanya managed to take on rent a small shed near Sivan theatre. A neat one. For Dev's factory. Father of one of her class mate owned it.

License and other permissions, was done with equal ease, as she knew many in Tirupur municipality.

"What are you going to name it Dev?"

Sukanya asked, on the way to Municipality office for applying for license.

"Sukanya Garments"

Dev answered with a smile.

"Don't be foolish Dev. Don't pull me into anything. Give it a globally acceptable and reachable name."

Dev scratched his head now, for a name. He had honestly wished to name it after Sukanya.

Many names flashed through his brain. And finally, when Sukanya gave him the application for filling up, he wrote:

Emerald Garments.

The name somehow had dawned on him.

Once the loan was sanctioned, she took him to a used hosiery machines dealer.

Ten basic sewing machines, 5 each of over lock, interlock and flat lock machines, two cutting tables, one large checking table, two ironing tables, one packing table and few other accessories.

Everything sealed for a bargain of five lakhs.

He had been sanctioned a term loan of five lakhs and a cash credit of another five lakhs.

His machines were ready and installed. He had roped in few of his cousins and their friends who were going to other companies for work.

The inauguration day came.

Function was very small. Dev's father was both happy and concerned. All his life, he had worked for some one. And according to him, that was easier than running on our own. He never thought of, or went behind big money. He made enough to pay for house rent, to bring provisions and occasional pleasantries for his family. He was able to attend all functions that came in family. He could pay for his occasional travels, to meet his family. He had all the time in the world to spend with his child and wife. What more one could want? He was satisfied with his means and life.

But now Dev was starting his own business. He was bit concerned about his son.

On the other hand, Dev's mother was happy for her son. At least him, he is going to break the jinx. He is starting his own company. Nobody ever did that in her family.

Sakthi's face kept flashing in her mind too. She didn't curse him, only because of his daughter.

Sukanya. The angel.

Sukanya came in and stayed for half an hour only. She had college.

"Stay here for today no" Dev begged. He wanted her by his side. The day he was starting. All these were her blessing only.

"It's ok Dev. Have to go. Got classes. And I can't be there all the time no. You have to start on your own now."

She smiled.

She was wearing blue jeans and a black top. Dev felt, she looked more beautiful that day.

" Do the switching on, and go. Sukanya, don't argue please. At least that much, for me."

" That is fine. But am not sure whether I am that auspicious person. "

She giggled.

"You are auspicious for me Sukanya. You saved me from rotting under some one. Now, come in please."

Dev's mother lighted the lamp. His father set everyone on their tables.

" Sukanya, please "

Dev, implored.

Sukanya, turned to the main switchboard, and switched on the power.

And the factory started running.

NINE

Life slowly found its rhythm.

Factory picked up operations quick enough. It was running to full capacity now. Day and night. It ran in two shifts to meet demand.

Fulchand & Sons, a big exporting company, gave him most of the orders.

Soon after opening of the factory, he had visited many exporting companies, scouting for orders.

And he visited Fulchand & Sons too.

Keval Chand Bafna. A Jain. Owner of Fulchand & Sons.

Dev could speak Hindi well, owing to his education in a central school. And that worked for him.

He conversed with Keval in Hindi. And Keval Chand instantly liked the boy.

"I will give you orders Dev. But be prompt. You know why small companies keep failing in Tirupur? After few initial orders, they start failing on deadlines. They do the work, but not within the delivery deadline. And thus they lose the trust and orders. Any help, you please call me. But never fail to meet deadlines. Important for you and important for me as well."

That was a great lesson for Dev. Never fail to meet deadlines.

Fulchand kept pumping in orders. And Dev kept supplying in time.

Slowly, he became their largest vendor.

And in two years, he went on to become an exporter himself.

That brought in larger margins to the company, with the same overhead. Compared to sub contract jobs.

Dev was able to move his factory to own building, in almost a year time. Better ventilated and ergonomically designed to smoothen the process flow.

More than two hundred employees now worked for the company. Dev got immensely busy. He rarely had time for rest.

But he continued to stay in that old rented house. That one room house.

No one is not judged by the size of their house. That is the beauty of Tamil nadu. So he could, while making all these money, continue his stay in that room.

He was happy there. Father still worked with Ramalingam. He came in the mornings, slept till afternoon. He will then come to factory with Dev's lunch. Sometimes Sarada, too will come with him. They were hardly getting to see him at home.

Some evenings, he still took that evening walk with Venkat Annan. Venkat Annan was the son of his land lord. It was the case ever since he was a boy. Venkat Annan, as Dev called him, used to take him for walks in the evenings. Mostly their walks took them to the New Bus stand. And they usually wound off their walks with one plate each of 'Kaalaan', a kind of mushroom based dish, from a street vendor, famous for that.

"You have grown too big Dev. No longer my little Dev, who waited for me to come back from work."

Venkat Annan said, looking both happy and concerned at the same time.

Dev looked up from his plate of Kaalaan.

Venkat Annan's eyes were moist.

"You came to stay in my house as a young boy. You were studying in sixth, if I remember correctly. From then, till now, You are with us. Don't know how long you will continue staying with us. When you are gone, I will miss you Dev."

Dev held Venkat Annan' arm.

But Dev didn't say anything. He knew his concerns were true.

Sukanya, was in her third year now. She called him once in a while, as she knew Dev was busy. Sometimes, she dropped into his office, to know how he was progressing.

"You are doing well, hero."

She said, one day, sipping on coffee. She was on a visit to his office.

Dev knew Sitaram Iyer, the aged accountant, was monitoring them from the corner seat.

He called in Karthik. Dev' s trusted man.

"Karthi, take care of production. No lags. And speed up the packing section. We need to be ready for cargo in few days. I will be back in one hour".

And they dashed out in his Volkswagen Jetta.

" You have time Sukanya?"

"Depends where actually you are thinking of going."

Sukanya laughed.

Dev realised how rare they met these days. He was busy in the company. And she was busy with her studies. Today she was having exam break. And Dev was the first thing that came to her mind.

"Your car is impressive." She remarked, after watching Dev drive, for some time.

"Can I drive"? She asked cutely.

"Of course Princess." Dev said smilingly, and stopped the car on the side of the road.

From there, Sukanya drove the car.

And she was driving pretty well. She grew up among flashy cars. A real princess.

They went to Marudamalai, a temple situated around sixty kilometers from Tirupur.

He wanted some time with Sukanya.

Car climbed up the hill with ease, and stopped just outside the old and majestic temple.

Lord Muruga. The deity.

It was almost three in the afternoon, and also a weekday. It accounted for fewer crowd.

After darshan, they sat on one of the steps.

A light breeze was teasing her hairs, and she kept pulling them back.

"What is it Dev? You look little dull. What happened?"

She asked him looking at his face. He was looking at his feet.

Dev, after a second of thought, looked up to face her.

"What did you get out of this Sukanya? You came; you helped me to start my own, and I am making money. Am not even thanking you enough. I am not even calling you often. "

Sukanya, smiled.

"I just showed you a way Dev. Rest everything, you did. I have enough money at home. You don't worry about that" she started laughing.

After a little pause, she asked.

"There is something else"

Sukanya teased him with a piercing look through the corner of her eyes.

" Am moving to Kerala, dear."

Dev said slowly.

Sukanya, just sat there in silence. Clearly shaken. Unable to speak.

TEN

" Too much of Sukanya"

Gayathri complained, handing me a cup of tea.

I smiled.

"Sukanya is the reason Dev reached where he is now. Can't ignore her Gachu"

"Still, am waiting for our sweet Revathy."

She said now, surprisingly blushing.

Girls and romance!

"They will meet gachu, when they are destined to meet."

"I hate writers, especially you"

She stormed into the kitchen, with a smirk.

ELEVEN

Few months back Dev's maternal uncle, Ramachandran, had visited him from Palakkad. Dev's native place. He was a marriage broker turned real estate agent.

Brokering marriages was turning into a high risk, low income career. Then, the real estate boom started. Many turned to real estate brokering, with much ease, as they already were having established contacts.

Ramachandran, was one of the many unregistered, unregulated, real estate agents in the country.

A segment sadly unregulated. A segment which turned many ordinary people into millionaires. Most of the time, they had the luxury of tax free income.

Ramachandran went straight inside Dev's cabin.

"Hi chandran uncle, long time. Hope you are fine"

Standing up from his seat, Dev greeted him and made him to sit opposite to him.

"You grew big Dev, and don't have time for us. Earlier, at least your father used to visit us. Now he also is not getting time to come.."

"..It has been months since I met my sister."

He said after a brief pause.

He looked concerned.

Dev knew he was speaking the truth.

Earlier, at least once in two months, his father used to visit most of his family. He visited them taking turns. He made sure, he reached everywhere. Sometimes he took Sarada and Dev too along with him. Sometimes, he went alone.

The respect he commanded from relatives.

That too, his father went everywhere, in bus.

He used to start early in the morning, on those days, on which he went visiting his family. And he used to return in time, to be present for night duty. He was punctuality personified.

This way, he ensured, he was in touch with his family roots and relatives. And they all in turn, loved him.

Now, Dev had a car. If only he wished, he could go to his native place with two hours of drive. Comfortably.

But he never could. Not that he never wished. Emerald Garments took up his time and energy, he had earlier, for other things in life.

"Tell me, Chandran uncle, what brought you here today. Have you been home? We still stay in the same house."

"No Dev. I thought of visiting you first. The very reason I come here is to ask you this; why are you still staying in the same house now?"

Dev looked at him with interest now. He liked this uncle among the few he had. Ramachandran had a great humour sense and sharp business acumen. Dev knew about his life as a street vendor in Chennai. Many years before. He made lots of money, but threw up everything in drinking. Now back in his native place, he was a changed man. Stopped drinking, and took to brokering. With his natural ability to do business and to make someone laugh, he was now making enough money.

"Dev, it is time you start giving some comforts to your parents. They have struggled all their lives. Let them live peacefully now."

"Uncle, what are you coming at? I am confused, honestly. They are very happy here."

"I meant, build your own home Dev. High time you did."

It was a new perspective, a new spark, for Dev.

He had never thought about it earlier.

He was making huge profits now. But investing it on a house never occurred to him.

" But don't do it here Dev. Not the right place for your parents or you to spend all life. I know Sarada. She surely wants to settle down in Palakkad at some point of time. With all of us now back there. She can visit temples, take bath in ponds, go for evening walks with sister in law's or friends. Your father too Dev, high time he is given a break. Let him spend rest of his life peacefully among us. The best thing you can do for them."

Dev now sat silently for some time, thinking.

"You may be thinking about your business. Dev, I can say with conviction that, with half the effort you are taking now, and half investment, you will earn double what you earn here. Only thing is that, you need to have some tact. And also someone, who can make business happen for you. For you, you have both."

He continued.

"Doesn't mean that you have to stop this all of a sudden. Continue this for some time. Start your operations in Palakkad. And find someone whom you can trust to run day to day business. Visit on crucial days. Stay one or two days here and come back home. You have the option of living well Dev. Only if you would think of it."

He made Dev thinking hard. After few minutes, Dev smiled, having made up his mind.

"How are the property rates in Palakkad, uncle?"

"Dev, now you got the point. Rates are very cheap now. But they will boom in another couple of years. Ten cents will now cost around three lakhs. You can build a nice home in that."

Dev smiled again, and started hitting few keys in computer. At the end, he took a printout. It was a map of Palakkad with important roads passing through it.

Ramachandran now watched him with some kind of amusement.

Dev drew few circles alongside NH 47 and two state highways.

He handed it over to Ramachandran.

"What I want is not ten cents of land uncle. I need few acres. I can invest around two crores. Get me the right land, and I will proceed."

He put extension plan of his company building in backburner now. Let Chandran Uncle come back with options. He will take a decision then.

Ramachandran sat speechless, and looked at the map given by Dev.

He had clearly underestimated Dev.

Two crores. Lots of money.

"You have got my business genes, Dev. I will get you some good deals, with that kind of money. See you Dev. And welcome to Palakkad soon."

With that, he walked towards the door.

TWELVE

"This is a huge house, Dev"

Sarada remarked, struggling to sink it in that it was being built for them. Dev had taken Sundaram and Sarada on a visit to the construction site in Palakkad.

For Sarada, even their one room house, back in Tirupur had too much of space for their family. Even if all three lie down on the floor, there was still enough space for an almirah.

But this was really huge.

3400 Sqft of splendor.

It had five bedrooms, open courtyard, patio, Pooja room, living room, dining room and kitchen. Everything was being done aesthetically. Dev had roped in the best architect from Kochi for its design. It followed a mix of European, contemporary and gothic style. And it stood on its own ground of 2 acres.

The house was being built inside around 100 acres of land he had acquired for a bargain. It was bordering NH 566. He could get it for substantially low rate as most of it was wet land. But, there was a small stretch of dry land in that. Dev decided to make his house on that piece of land.

Rest of the land was earmarked for re classification from wet land to dry land. These lands were remaining of large fields, taken over by government for developing National

Highway. Since their water flows were blocked at various places, farmers left it without cultivation. For many years now. Dev, wanted everything to be done according to law. He didn't like to take short cuts. He wanted rest of the land to be declassified as wet land. Then only he thought of starting his operations there.

"Son, why you are going for this land development permit and all? Nobody has ever taken permit for subdivision of land here in Palakkad. Wasting time Dev. Divide, sell and get lost from that place."

Ramchandran asked one day.

He had brought files to Dev's office, for onward submission at Panchayath. Dev's signature were required in many places.

"Uncle, have you heard of KPBR 2011? Kerala panchayath Building Rules. There it clearly says that before subdividing any property, you have to get approval from concerned authorities. No shortcuts, Chandran uncle. Please. "

Dev, smiled at him.

Ramachandran looked at Dev with appreciation now. He clearly has done his homework.

Since his commitment, Ramachandran had arranged few lands for Dev. Some of them Dev resold for huge profits. Three pieces of land, which Dev thought to be prime, were not sold. The layout permits were being applied for these three lands. Dev had his plans.

Karthi came in with some files after Ramachandran had left. Export and clearing house related documents. Boxes were ready to be dispatched to Chennai for shipment. They were being moved next day.

"How is your mother now Karthi?"

Dev asked him while signing the documents. Karthi had gone home the previous day, soon after his lunch. His mother was not well.

"She is fine now sir. She had slight variations in ECG. But doctor said nothing to worry as blood test proved normal. Still, she is on medication. "

"Take care of her Karthi. Whenever there is a need, go home and see her. Don't wait for my approval."

"Thank you sir."

He smiled and went out.

Karthi was a graduate. He was a very honest guy too. Dev knew he could trust him. He had larger roles to play, if Dev shifted operations to Palakkad.

"How are you Sitaram sir? How is your daughter doing now? Last you told, she had fever and was hospitalised. "

"She is fine now sir. Hospitals in Pune are really good. She got well in three days. I was concerned as she was second time pregnant now".

"Let them be safe Sitaram sir. Convey my regards when she calls you next. Last time she came here, I couldn't meet."

He just smiled at him with gratitude. With age, people become wise and graceful. And grateful too.

Dev now walked out of his office, and started climbing the stairs to first and second floor of his company. Somehow, he missed walking up. Past few months he has been too preoccupied to look after production floors. That day, he decided to take a break. Soon, this will be an once in a month affair. Or may be even longer.

He went to the second floor first. The cutting, tailoring and checking sections functioned in the second floor. Arun and Ramdas, both his cousins, rose up from their tables and came to him.

"Hi Dev, long time you came here. All fine?"

He hugged them.

"All fine dears. Just that I have too many other things to look after too. Since you guys are here, I need not come up here often, just to see everything is ok; right no?"

He laughed.

It was true. Arun and Ramdas were a comfort for him. They managed production even when Dev never asked them to do. They both had a sense of ownership. And when they were around, even Karthi didn't meddle there much.

He went to each table in turn and talked to them, for a minute each. Everyone was happy and doing well. They were the people who were contributing in big way for his success.

He walked down to first floor.

Karthi was busy there, looking after packing. He came running.

"Sir, anything?"

"Nothing particular Karthi, just wanted to have a look."

He answered, while walking in.

He went and stood near ironing table. Govindasamy Anna was ironing with heavy iron box. Dev had been watching him ironing cloths without breaks for hours. Although he worked on piece rate, his dedication could never be questioned. There were three more ironing guys. Few joined recently. All were happy to see Dev.

He looked at the packing section. All were busy putting garments into carton boxes and packing and sealing. Some new girls looked at him through corner of their eyes and smiled between them. Elder ladies seemed to admonish them with their eyes.

He walked out into the verandah and stood looking out over the skyline of Tirupur. Many small and big buildings had sprouted out all over.

He looked towards Sivan Theatre. Earlier it was visible without much effort. Now he had to crane his neck a bit to see it.

How many days, how many evenings, he has been there, as a kid; going to cinema, with wide happy eyes, along with Venkat Annan.

He will be leaving Tirupur Soon. Construction of his house at Palakkad was now finished and ready to move. He will be visiting Tirupur only once in a while. He was going to miss this place.

He missed Sukanya Now.

The one who made all this possible. The one who saved him from the ditches.

A dry hot Breeze flew in from outside and unsettled his hairs. While he was pulling it back in place, he saw Sukanya sliding in, on her scooty.

He, though happy, was bit nervous. He will have to break it to Sukanya today.

THIRTEEN

"Did you love Sukanya?"

I asked Dev. We were taking a walk inside his Emerald luxury Villas project, just outside his Villa No. 45. I used to visit him sometimes, whenever he was free, just to get facts correct.

Dev smiled.

"Bharath sir, you don't love God. You worship him from a distance. The feeling is different. And is on a much higher plane than love. Sukanya, is god to me. She gave me this life."

Dev was walking, looking down, lost in thought.

"What about Sukanya? Did she love you?"

I asked him after a pause.

That question gave a chill to Dev.

Why did this never occur to him? What if she did? Probably she did not. Or did she?

"Bharath Sir, I never thought about it; honestly."

He fell silent. Sweat started flooding his handsome face, even in that cool evening.

FOURTEEN

Everything was being moved to its right places. Minor adjustments in their positions. Dev wanted everything to be perfect. He had handcrafted this house, brick by brick, corner by corner. From the interior plants to be placed in the courtyard, to the colour of the walls. Everything handpicked and set according to Dev's wishes.

The transport vehicle from Tirupur had gone back. He had planned to leave everything they had, there in Tirupur only. But he couldn't deny his mother bringing something from her personal collections. She had to have her memories.

Few of his employees, and his two cousins were staying back for night. They wanted to make sure Dev didn't fall short of anything. Also, they were happy to be in his house. They had planned to go back early in the morning.

Some works were still going on. Ramachandran was personally overseeing the works. He had also arranged a maid for helping Dev's mother. She was in the kitchen preparing for dinner.

Sarada, lighted the lamps in Pooja room. She kept one lighted lamp at the centre of the sitout too, the flame facing east.

She was really happy. Sundaram was happy too. No matter how much they would discuss between them, they could never get tired of talking how beautifully their house has come up. And how huge.

Dev was thinking of the previous day. An emotion packed day.

Sukanya had visited them in the evening. Dev noted how much Sarada liked Sukanya. Her eyes would light up whenever she saw Sukanya. Sundaram too loved this girl. She grew up holding his hands. He would never forget all those walks to school.

"After going there, don't become a thorough mallu, Dev. Always looking at coconut tree and counting the coconuts." She giggled.

Dev turned to her. She was trying hard to hide her emotions. And look normal.

"I will be coming often, Sukanya. I still have my factory here. But that may be twice in a month. Those construction projects in Palakkad will eat up my time. You know that I am new to that field. That is the first reason why I wanted to shift to Palakkad. Too much of money involved there. It is very easy to lose money and quality, if you are not there personally. "

Dev felt Sukanya was listening, but not taking in. He knew nothing he would tell Sukanya would comfort her.

Sarada brought in coffee for them.

"What are you planning to do after your engineering, Sukanya?" Dev asked, to change topic.

"No plans Dev. May be civil services. Or on the easier side, I will get a foreign visa and study some stupid course and settle down abroad. No plans of continuing here in Tirupur, Dev."

Dev knew, she was good in her studies.

"You will do well Sukanya. And you have this knack of turning everything into gold. Look at me." Dev laughed, with an effort.

Sukanya smiled now.

"You are gold, by birth. I just rubbed off the dust. Don't be modest." She giggled now.

She left when it was getting too late for her.

Venkat returned from factory very ealy that day. He came in with his mother. She loved Dev's family. She started crying, as she started talking to Sarada.

Venkat held Dev by his arm.

"Come Dev. Let's go for a walk. "

And they walked out into Tirupur. They walked along the road lined with little provision stores, well lit bakeries giving out loud music, and big temples. They passed Sivan Theatre and Dev's new company building behind that. They were walking automatically towards new bus stand. Their legs were programmed to walk in that direction. It was always like that. Ever since Dev was a kid.

People were hurrying on the roads. Some were coming back from their shifts. Some others were rushing madly to join their shifts. Girls in half saris, their hair tied in cross knots, and fresh jasmine flowers pinned in place with their hair. Men in trousers, with full sleeve shirts buttoned at the wrists, tucked out, and sandals. And that ubiquitous Reynolds pen in their pockets. Some rushing in group, some rushing alone. The mayhem, which was called Tirupur.

He loved this city like this.

Today, both didn't feel like eating anything.

"You came here as a small kid, Dev. " Venkat repeated.

"And grew up in front of me. You are like my little brother only. Do come home, whenever you visit your factory."

"And I won't be coming with you tomorrow to Palakkad. Can't bear that. Please go safe Dev. Look after your parents.

They are like my elder brother and sister. "

Dev held Venkat's hand now.

"Don't come Annan. Even I can't bear that. I will keep coming Venkat Annan. Don't worry."

Early next morning, before Tiupur could wake up, they left the city. Family went in the car. Their belongings and workers accompanied them on a mini truck.

FIFTEEN

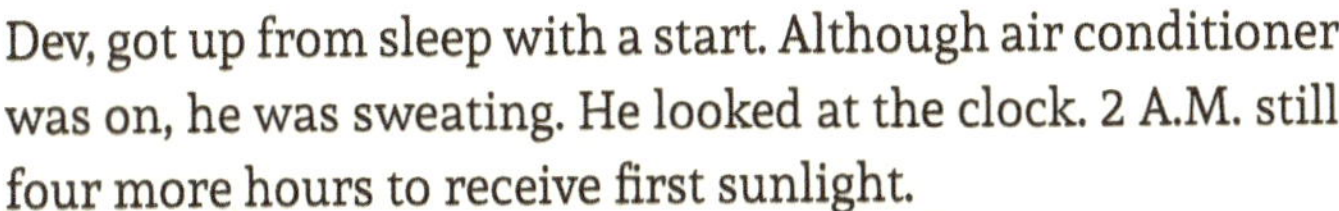

Dev, got up from sleep with a start. Although air conditioner was on, he was sweating. He looked at the clock. 2 A.M. still four more hours to receive first sunlight.

Yesterday was the peak of his life. The launch of Emeralad Mall. He had nothing more to achieve in life now. For the 20 year old labourer kid, who got slapped in the dingy office room, he had come a long way.

Of all his ventures, this was the most taxing one. Lots of brains went into it. Lots of designs and lots of funds.

And finally, the mall was launched. And by the feel of it, it was going to be a big money spinner.

Since he arrived in Kerala four years before, he had been toiling hard for getting this online. He had other villa projects too, going on simultaneously. But nothing was bigger and prestigious than this one.

Today, though he lost his sleep, he felt relieved. He walked out from his bedroom to balcony. There was considerable traffic through National Highway, even at this hour. He sat there, watching in silence for some time.

Where will be Sukanya now? It was quite some time since he talked to Sukanya. Initially, she used to call daily. Slowly, as Dev got busier, the calls got rarer. And for the past one year, he realised with a shock, he had not talked to Sukanya. Can he call her now?

Today, here he was; Dev of today. Standing tall in life. All because of her. All because, she made him to think beyond his means. At this time of night, sitting peaceful, and free. Can he call her?

He fumbled with phone for few minutes. Something held him back. He didn't dial.

He went back to sleep.

Next day, his first stop was the mall. He got in just before the opening hours. He wanted to be among the crowds, un noticed. He wanted to walk among them through the length and breadth of the concrete garden he had made. He wanted to share their happiness, their excitement, and their feelings.

It was like the opening day. Crowd poured in. They thronged each and every store. The efforts he had taken, building it from scratch, getting the dealers, and store operators. The entertainment zone cost crores. But never mind. The customers and kids were having a ball.

He walked among the crowd, slowly, taking in the scenes. His employees, on recognising him, wished from distances. He kept smiling back.

The thing that was taking most of his efforts and time was now done. It was now time for him to sit back and relax.

He walked to his cabin on the third floor.

Devanarayan. Chairman and Managing Director. The name board proudly announced.

He walked into his plush office.

Vasudev, his friend, driver and personal assistant, was waiting on the settee. He stood up on seeing Dev.

"Vasu, please sit."

He told Vasu, while settling down on his chair. "Where is Baby bro?" He asked, with a smile.

Vasu smiled. "He must be here any time. Yesterday, after everything, he boozed like anything." Vasu started laughing.

Dev smiled too. Let them have an off day mood. They all worked like hell for this Mall. It was time to unwind, for them too.

"Vasu, once Baby bro comes, we will go to our kallekkad site. High time, we start focusing on our villa projects again. We all were too much behind this Mall. I feel, things are going loose at that end."

"Don't worry sir. I was in touch with Manoj, all the time. He is taking care of it well. And we are expecting to get clearance for the project by today. He is in touch with Pirayiri Panchayath."

And some one opened the door.

It was Baby. Dev's face widened in a smile.

"Come in Baby bro. Hope your feet can feel the earth" he laughed.

Baby cut a shy smile. For his age, he was too shy, especially when someone commented on his drinking sessions.

Vasu was laughing too.

Baby came and sat opposite to Dev.

"Dev brother, hope everything is going well here. Hope there is no hiccups." Baby asked.

Baby, although he drank hard, was very meticulous in works. He came into his projects as a part time plumber and electrician. Now he has become an invariable part of Dev's inner circle. He went with Dev, wherever he went.

Just then, Vasu's phone rang.

"Manoj", he said looking at the flashing name on his screen. He attended the call.

His face lit up. He cut the call.

"The high court order did the job. We got the development permit." He smiled at Dev.

Dev looked up in prayers. And then looked at both Baby and Vasu with a smile. Crores of his money was locked in that land at Kallekkad. He has been waiting to hear this for months now.

"Not a bad day Vasu. Come let us go to kallekkad."

With that, Dev walked out. Baby and Vasu followed him.

SIXTEEN

Dev's black BMW X7 entered into Emerald project campus at Kallekkad. The three got down and walked to the camp office. Manoj was sitting, cramped with files and drawings.

He stood up on Seeing Dev and team.

"Finally, Manoj. You did it. Really a Great job."

Dev sat opposite to him, and congratulated Manoj.

"Thank you sir. But all credit goes to the advocate. He won the case for us. Judgement was clear. I only had to ensure we present a clear drawing and submit necessary papers."

Dev now, reached for the drawings in Manoj's hand and looked at it for some time.

Manoj now continued in an apologetic tone.

"I didn't want to trouble you, as you were too occupied with the Mall sir. So I directly submitted the drawings to Town planner, without putting up to you."

Dev waved aside his apology with a slight movement of hand.

" That is fine Manoj. Don't feel bad about it. You are the expert. I depend on you. And I know, you are doing a great job."

"And these drawings. As always, neat and well laid out. They meet my instructions and expectations. All plots of minimum ten cents size. All are well-spaced and square.

Road is wide enough, with a width of ten meters. There is enough common space. There are a total of hundred and forty plots in ten acres of land. Whatever it lacks, it is never going to lack space and ergonomics. Good work Manoj."

"And now what, Manoj?"

Dev looked at Manoj.

"We have one final appointment with Town planner sir. He wanted to see a sample drawing of the villa we are going to construct in it. Just his personal interest. Nothing to do with development permit. "

" So just waiting for your first whistle, and the game is on."

Manoj looked at Dev, smilingly.

Dev was happy. He loved his team. Gem. Each one of them.

"Then start tomorrow Manoj. We have leased a quarry near Alathur. Tell them to roar loud from tomorrow. "

He turned to Vasu now.

"Vasu, please tie up with quarry guys. Manoj will be new to them. They should supply outside, only when we satisfy Manoj's appetite. Right from tomorrow."

"Ok sir ". Vasu took his command happily. That was him. Tell him anything. And he takes it as his own personal job.

Next second, he was ordering someone on phone.

"No outside supply, until I tell. All production to Kallekkad, from tomorrow. No lapses."

Everything set up for tomorrow.

Just then, Manoj's phone rang again.

He was talking to someone in a low tone, and was rubbing his forehead in disgust.

"Ok Colonel Sir. I will bring it. Somehow."

He finally disconnected the call, saying those words.

"What is it Manoj? Tensed about something?"

Dev asked him.

"Nothing sir. One of our customer. A Colonel. Our Chandranagar Project customer."

"I know him Manoj. I had met him the other day. A true Colonel."

Dev smiled. " what he wants now?"

"Now he is in state bank loan processing center sir, for his documentation. Big loan. Eighty lakhs. Bank is leaving nothing to chance. Want every document perfect."

"That is fine from the bank point of view Manoj. They are financing the purchase. It is public money. Their concern is justified. Anything now left from our side?"

"Yes sir. I missed the building approval and approved drawings, when I handed him over the documentation set. I whatsapped the documents to the processing officer. They sanctioned the loan, on condition that the original set may be produced on documentation day. Today is his documentation. He is already half done. Now they asked him for the drawings. And he got stuck. Somehow I missed. Sorry sir"

"That is not a problem Manoj. I personally know their Assistant General Manager. A very young man for his rank. Energetic. Meet him and take my name. He will help you."

"That is the catch sir" Manoj drew on. "Now I have that appointment with town planner too"

he scratched his chin.

Dev got the point.

"Give that set to me Manoj. I will handover. As such, I have nothing better to do. I will also have the honour of meeting Colonel sir once again. "

"Sir.." Manoj hesitated.

"Vasu, take that file. We are going."

Dev stood up and turned to the door. When Vasu's name is taken, Manoj knew, it is final.

" Vasu Bhai, take these"

Manoj handed over the files to Vasu, as Vasu smiled at him affectionately.

" Meet the town planner Manoj. I will take care of this." Vasu assured him, and followed Dev and Baby out of the room.

BMW came to life once again, and sped towards, the state bank processing center, at Fort Maidan.

Little did Dev know, that journey will change the tempo of his life.

SEVENTEEN

World was just coming out of the first wave of Covid. Every single industry was hit badly. And so did Real estate. Deals were rare. People were scared to spend big. All were in some sort of confusion. When this will all stop? When this will all end?

Everyone put big decisions on hold.

No new cars, no new homes. Just pull on life, without getting infected. That was the general feeling everywhere.

Dev, knew the value of such a big deal now. It should not get spoiled just because of petty issues. That is why he himself volunteered. Not that he was having any kind of dull period. Still, it gave him a kind of kick that his projects were selling, when everyone else were laid off. Thanks to quality of his projects, location and value for money it offered to customers.

Vasu parked the car in the parking space at the backyard of the bank campus. The three walked to the entrance of the Loan processing center. In fact, it was a Centralised Processing center. It was the nerve center of credit activities of the bank in the district. Loan proposals came from branches located all over the district. These were scrutinised, legal opinions of title documents were taken, valuations were done, processed and sanctioned at the CPC. Documentations and disbursements were also done at the

CPC. A proper loan hub of the bank.

Most of Dev's projects were approved by bank already, which meant no legal and valuations part for his clients. It was all done once and kept ready for all his customers.

Save this particular project, one unit of which was now being bought by Colonel Raghunath sir. It was a new project. The project had been submitted for bank's approval and was in process. Colonel couldn't wait that long. He had only few days leave left and wanted the registration to be done in that small window of time. So, separate legal and valuations were arranged for his plot and house.

These were all taken care of by Manoj and team in normal case. Dev never interfered in those things. And he didn't have time too. He was not a follower of micro management in any way. He liked to delegate and empower. Each person in his fold were each a business unit. Each of them was capable of taking decisions. And all of them were empowered to do so.

Today, he was unwinding. After the Mall inauguration, he felt light. He wanted to step out. He just wanted to loiter around, be with friends, and roam in sunlight. So he willingly took on the responsibility of handing over the documents at CPC. He clearly was having fun. He thought of meeting the Colonel and also Viswanath sir, who was the present AGM of CPC. He was feeling light and happy.

Security person recognised Dev, when he lowered his mask. Morning papers were full of the Emerald Mall and Dev. One had even done a half page on Dev.

He came running to Dev.

"Good morning sir. Anything sir?"

Dev smiled affably.

"Viswanath sir is in?" He asked him.

"He is out sir. Chief Manager is in. If anything you can meet him sir. Shall I take you in?"

"Thank you Ram sir", Dev said, reading name from his name tally. "Nothing much. One of my customer is in, doing documentation. I just wanted to take few papers to him. May I go in?"

"Of course sir"

And he got Dev's signature and details in Visitors register.

Security person was baffled. Morning papers were singing saga of this young man, and here he was, carrying some papers himself. He would have loved to picturise Dev in khaki shorts and fancy shirt, vacationing in Maldives. May be with his private jet basking in sunlight in the background. He had seen it in films. Big bosses and travels. They never worked, did they? He kept thinking about Dev. Success gets others think about you, even in your absence.

Dev and Vasu walked in. Baby chose to stay outside. He may wish to take a puff. Dev guessed. So he allowed him to stay back.

It was a different world altogether, which presented before them, as they opened the main door. The banking hall had around thirty counters to the right, in which officers were all bent on their own files. Each one handled a particular part in the journey of a loan file. Some did processing, some did sanctioning, some did coordination and some did hard recoveries of bad loans. He was once briefed by Viswanath sir, about the process flow. It was before two years, when he had come with a customer.

He looked into AGM's cabin. It was empty. He was out. Lights in his cabin, punctually switched off. A man with extra-terrestrial capability levels. That was Viswanath sir. And an AGM rank for him at this young age was not all surprising to Dev.

Now he looked towards Documentation table. He could see the Colonel and his wife, appending their signatures, on a pile of papers, bent and too absorbed on the papers they were signing. They didn't notice Dev entering or the world around them working like humanoids.

Dev could not see the officer sitting opposite to Mr and Mrs Colonel, who was taking their documentation. A pillar blocked his view.

And, slowly, he could make out a hand, turning pages of the documents set.

Very fair, and beautiful. A lady officer. The smart watch on her hand in direct contrast to her skin colour, shouting out loud, how fair she was. Dev started walking towards them. Vasu, followed in silence.

Now, she started coming into Dev's view.

First, her hair, cut into layers, and kept open. Flowing beautifully over her shoulders.

Then her eye lashes. Dev had never seen such big eye lashes.

And her eyes. And she was smiling beautifully, talking something to Colonel.

Thank god, she chose not wear a mask. Or maybe she kept aside it for that moment. Wearing a mask all day, from morning till night, was a difficult option. You tend to re fix it all time, pulling it here there and everywhere. Whatever, she didn't wear one that time. Dev was only too happy about that.

Dev had her full view now, from where he had reached.

She was wearing a lime yellow top, and a light blue jeans. The dress lifted up her poise and grace manifolds.

Dev realized now, she was really beautiful. Somehow, for the first time after many years, his legs felt light, with nervousness. He didn't know why.

He slowly approached them. Unconsciously staring at her.

Her name card was on the table.

Revathy. Deputy Manager.

And now she lifted up her head only to find Dev, staring.

How gracefully girls take in, when some one stares at them. That abnormality is usual to them may be. They were trained to buy it. A kind of AI. Acquire it as you grow up as a girl.

She cut her smile midway, and looked at Dev with questioning glances. Dev felt butterflies fluttering in his stomach.

"Yes?"

She asked. A drawing, sweet voice.

Dev forgot what he was. Or why he came here at all.

Colonel, surprisingly didn't see him either. He was signing it with a perfection and focus of picking up mines in a battle field. Steady and unwavering.

" Wanted to handover some documents" All that Dev could stammer out was this.

Without head or tail!

" Please go and wait there, let me finish with these people. Will call you" she said, surprisingly with a stern voice for her graceful outlook.

"But.." Dev tried to explain.

"Please wait" Her voice was now more stern. She pointed at the empty chairs.

Vasu made an angry movement from behind. He could never take an insult to Dev.

Dev stopped him, holding his hand. Thankfully, she didn't notice his movement. Dev didn't want to spoil the show.

With a faint smile, and a slight movement of head to say yes, he turned to take seat for the waiting customers. It was just in front of AGM's cabin.

"What sir? You mean to say she didn't recognise you? She don't read newspapers?" Vasu was flaring up.

Dev smiled at him.

"She may not have Vasu. And certainly, not with my mask on. And just sit back and enjoy the fun. Long time, since I have been kept waiting in a lounge. Let us bask in glory."

The documentation went on for some time more. Colonel was now seen taking up phone and dialing Manoj. He was angry that the documents were not given to him still.

"No mistake sir. Dev sir himself carried it there. He must be there only"

Manoj was heard saying over the mobile speaker.

Colonel was now seen throwing searching glances all over. And he now turned sharp enough to look directly behind him.

His face lighted up instantly.

"Mr. Dev..." He stood up and came to him. Dev too stood up from his chair.

"Why all this trouble of carrying it yourself Dev? I feel bad that I made you to do it. " Colonel apologized.

"No problem Colonel sir. I wished to see you also. And today I am free. So there are no issues as such. Manoj alerted me in time. I came in long back." Dev said, smiling.

He saw Revathy watching him now. She seemed to feel now that something was not right.

"Then why you were waiting Dev. "I feel very bad that you were waiting silently for me."

"No issue at all Colonel sir. I came to your side. You were busy signing. "

Now Revathy got up and came to them. Gracefully like a wave. She understood she had made some mistake in recognizing this person. Even Colonel sir was talking with respect to him.

"Sorry Colonel Sir. He came to me. I only told him to wait for some time. He came for you?"

Now Colonel turned to her.

"I wonder what you read in the mornings young lady. Don't you recognise Dev, Devanarayan, of Emerald Builders & Emerald Mall? Whole state is talking about him now"

Revathy froze on the spot. She understood now. His face had looked somewhat familiar to her. May be his mask betrayed her. Now she recognised him well.

"I am really sorry Dev sir, I didn't recognise you." She said in a very apologetic tone.

"Not an issue madam. You were only doing your duty well."

Dev handed over the documents to her seemingly frozen hand.

"Ok Colonel Sir. Namaste madam." He wished both Mr & Mrs Colonel and then smiled at Revathy.

She was standing still, as if she had lost her ear balance.

Dev, now turned and walked out. Vasu, followed him, not entirely satisfied.

"What kind of young men, this country produce. He would have made a fine Service officer. A thorough gentleman."

The Colonel muttered proudly to Mrs. Colonel.

Revathy, stood there, head turning now. She felt immensely guilty.

EIGHTEEN

That evening, Dev was too lazy to hit the Gym. A kind of laziness, that gets you out the next ball, after you have scored a century; after you have done the last shades of the painting; after the last words of a poem has been written to perfection.

Instead he chose to take a cool walk. He had dismissed Vasu and Baby to their homes, an hour before. For months they were regularly going home late, sometimes even past midnight too. The Mall was taxing on their time too. But now Dev decided that, he will send them off at proper time. They too have their families to look after. Poor guys.

Many were taking a walk inside the Emerald campus. And some kids were cycling. It was a well laid out gated community housing project. Wide roads, shade trees on either side of the roads, park for the kids and some small shopping centers. Most recently the Mall. Everything inside.

Few of them who recognised Dev, smiled at him. He smiled and waved back. May be they were seeing him for the first time. Though he lived inside the campus, he was rarely out on foot inside the campus. They all knew Dev lived there. But they never saw him going out or coming in.

He decided to take a long walk. Today he had plenty of time. He liked the feeling of walking alone. It ensured some time for himself.

He walked out of the campus into the National Highway. Traffic was flowing left and right vehemently. He kept to the foot path. Dev liked the cool breeze. He took in the faces that crossed him; some smiling, some unfamiliar, and some in deep thoughts. He kept going away from the hustle and bustle of traffic winding into Emerald Mall. His own baby. He wanted to be away from all the noise. He walked silently.

Few of them who saw him walking as they passed in their vehicles, and who were close enough to him, called him on phone.

"There is nothing serious. I am just taking my evening walk" he laughed and replied to each enquiring calls.

He must have come five kilometers towards the centre of the town. Traffic was getting uncomfortably heavy to walk. He saw the Hitech Towers defining the night sky. All luxury flats. He knew the developer personally. Many times he had sought Dev's partnership in building flats. But somehow, Dev didn't like flats. He never liked the idea of living in nests in air. And so he never built flats himself. And Dev, always excused him out of Flat projects with Hitech.

Now he turned and started walking towards his home.

Almost 7.30PM now. Mom must be worried. He realised how less time he was getting to spend time with his father and mother.

How business isolates you from the rest of the world. You end talking with the people who matter most in business. Not those people who actually matter in your lives. Not even your parents. You live some kind of avatar life. Transported to a different world altogether. Coming back to the real world only once a while. Emotionally too drained out, to respond in your real world.

Dev felt his father's comforting hands on his cheeks, the day he was slapped. And his mother's tears. He suddenly wished to be among them. He started walking fast.

And his phone rang now. Someone saw me again? He took out his mobile from the pocket of his jeans.

A new number was flashing on the screen.

Dev thought for a second whether to pick it up or not.

Another call for funds? from one of the political reps? He used to get calls regularly for funds from political parties. A procession to be organised, a meeting to be arranged, a mass wedding to be conducted, etc, etc.

"Dev sir, you know it is difficult to run a party with membership fees alone. We depend on favours from people like you. And you know that there are not many like you in Palakkad to whom we can turn to."

They would grin.

Dev had no option but to satisfy their requirements. With some limits though. You need all kind of support when you are doing real estate. Everything works here on political tie ups.

The call had died out. Dev left a sigh of relief. After a moment of pause, the phone rang again. Same number again. Probably the caller hesitated for a second before deciding to call again.

Something convinced Dev to attend that call now.

"Hello.."

A sweet voice came out from the other side. Dev felt it was somehow familiar.

"Hello, Dev sir?"

The girl on the other side, asked again, when Dev didn't respond for a second.

"Yes, Dev here" he answered now.

"Sir, it is me, Revathy. From State Bank. We met in the morning."

Dev now understood why the voice sounded familiar.

"Yes, Revathy mam, it is a surprise actually. Please tell me, anything needed from our side?"

Dev suspected that they again left out something in connection with Colonel's documentation.

"Dev sir, I am really sorry. I was rude to you when you came in the morning. I didn't know that it was you." Her voice was now sweeter than the morning.

He had forgotten about the morning. He had not even taken it as an insult. He was just enjoying his off day. An ordinary person living his life. Waiting for everything came by their nature. Nothing big for a commoner. They were kept waiting, for everything, all their lives.

Dev felt happy though. Somehow, this girl had stayed in his mind, since this morning.

It was her eyes. He remembered now.

"Revathy mam, that is fine. I know your work pressures. Excess Volumes of work sometimes make you behave rude. It is quite understandable. If this is of any consolation to you, I didn't feel bad at all."

"But I felt guilty even after you left sir. Colonel was telling me how nice a person you are. Even our AGM, when he knew about it was somewhat angry on me. I am really sorry again, Dev sir."

"That was not at all a problem Revathy mam. Please don't worry. But how did you get my personal number? I don't think I have given my personal number to Colonel or even your AGM sir."

" Trade secret, Dev sir."

She giggled. Dev laughed too.

" Well, Won't hide it from you. Lifted it from the visitors book" she laughed heartily.

Dev now remembered that the security person had taken down his details in Visitors book, when he went there in the morning. Somehow, inadvertently, he may have given his personal number then.

"You are smart Revathy Mam" Dev laughed now.

"Revathy. Just Revathy is enough sir. And I know I am smart. Thank you anyway Dev sir. I didn't know that you big people attended calls. I was expecting some proud PA asking me to wait."

Dev felt touched.

"Is it ok if I save your number Revathy? I don't have the luxury of a visitor's book" Somehow, he felt brave enough to ask her.

"Yes"...she said after a pause. "And thanks once again. Good night Dev sir."

" Dev, just Dev. Don't make me so feel so old Revathy. I am just twenty six."

"Oh ok, Good night Dev.." she wished, giggling. And the other side fell silent.

Dev never felt this much better. Smiling, he started walking back at a faster pace.

NINETEEN

Dev was now too big to be trapped in Tirupur. Still, he didn't shut down Emerald Garments. That was his start. That was Sukanya's gift. That gave him this life.

He visited the factory once in two months. It was being managed by his cousins now. They gave him daily reports through WhatsApp. Karthi was no more in his service. Though that was a big jolt to Dev, his cousins stepped in. They were capable of looking after production. Sitaram sir looked after accounts. Office was managed by a new girl, Keerthana. A post graduate in business management. She took care of all correspondences. Dev still attended important buyer meetings. They were usually arranged in Coimbatore. So he didn't have to travel all the way to Tirupur, just for attending the meetings.

Still, there were unavoidable things like statutory papers to be signed, authorisations for spending on infrastructure, employee welfare decisions and quality control, which required Dev's personal attention. He made his travels, clubbing as far as possible, two or three things.

Each visit to Tirupur was special to Dev. Journey back to the place where it all started. Each was a nostalgic journey.

But he missed Sukanya whenever he visited Tirupur. He tried her number twice or thrice, but the number now didn't exist. He didn't have the will to go to her home searching for her. Thinking of Sakthi to him was like thinking about slithery insects. It gave him a kind of nauseating feeling.

He enquired in his company whether Sukanya came there after her had shifted. She had never come. She had kind of vanished from his life. Dev got sad and guilty whenever he thought about Sukanya. Only, if he had attended her calls. Honestly, Dev wished to call her back. But it never happened. With each deals, he got busier. New layouts, new projects, new deals and finally the Mall. He had his bag full.

Someday, Dev thought, Sukanya will apparate in front of him. He was sure of that. Whenever, he really wanted her. Whenever, she wished. She was feminine divinity to him. Capable of anything.

Dev had developed this new habit of checking WhatsApp status updates. It started after he talked to Revathy. He had saved her number, and was getting to see updates from her. To think, he never cared to check updates, before Revathy.

Girls make men do weird things...!!!

Revathy was one of them, who put up regular updates. She posted each and every fraction of her life. She was this happy going, worry free girl. A transfer in her office, a temple visit, a new sari, parents' wedding anniversary; everything Dev knew through her status updates.

Dev was one of those guys, who was too shy to take the first step. With each passing day, Dev was getting to know more about Revathy. What her interests were, which book she was currently reading, the places she visited, who all she worked with and so on. With each updates, Dev was growing fonder of her. She looked cuter and sweeter to him each passing day. With each passing day, and with each of her posts, she grew bigger on Dev. But he never dared.

And Dev hopelessly kept looking for her status updates, almost every minute.

He kept glued on to the mobile screen, when he travelled from home to office, office to mall, during tea breaks, during staff meetings, while having breakfast or lunch, or even when he was on bed to catch few hours' sleep.

What he got out of it, he didn't know. He was just happy knowing her. Her smiles, her dresses, her writings, and everything about her.

He got two or three more documentations of his clients at state bank CPC. He had the temptation of going to CPC and checking on them. May be he will get to see Revathy once again. But he resisted the temptation always. He thought he would look foolish.

Vasu was pretty amused the way Dev was spending time on phone these days. Generally, while on drives, Dev used to talk to Vasu. He used to talk about many things. But off late, Dev was almost silent. Whenever Vasu observed him through Rear View mirror, he would find Dev sitting silently, with his eyes hooked on to mobile screen. Something is not right. Vasu guessed.

Even Sarada and Sundaram were realising the change in Dev. Sarada used to talk lot, whenever she got her son, within her range. She would walk behind him all the time, telling him about their relatives, who all called her that day, what was happening in their lives, how Sundaram had been stupid enough to do that and do this and so on. Sarada was a devoted wife. She found cuteness in everything Sundaram did. Everything was a story to be told to her Son.

But these days Dev never responded back. He cut short their talk with an hm or yes or no. He would still smile at them. But he was in some other world. Sarada knew her son was not completely with her now. She would look meaningfully at Sundaram.

"Anything worrying you Dev?"

His father asked one evening when Dev returned. He could never stand his son suffering.

"Nothing Dad. Everything is good."

Dev replied smilingly, and vanished to his room in top floor.

That particular day, Dev was feeling sleepless for some unknown reason. May be the coffee he had had foolishly with the dinner. He was just not able to get sleep.

He walked to the balcony, and sat in the bamboo couch. Traffic was flowing gracefully over national highway. He realised how graceful the traffic looks, from a distance. Darkness, intermittently cut open by head lights of incoming and outgoing vehicles. It was a pretty sight. You only see the festival of lights. No deafening sound. The same traffic looks maddening when you observed from close.

How things change when perspectives change...

He looked around. The other villas in the gated community sprouted out from darkness, basking in faint lights. It made a pretty sight in darkness. More than one hundred fifty villas, arranged beautifully over a vast span of land, and basking in individual outdoor lamps. All solar ones. It was silence everywhere. He would have loved to walk around, if only he had someone else to walk with. Alone, he would look like a fool, and that too at this hour. He now saw one of the securities taking rounds of the big campus on a bicycle. So things worked. Dev felt happy.

It was past midnight now. Involuntarily he took out his mobile phone. His fingers touched the famous green chat icon. And by habit, he touched the status tab automatically.

What a surprise. His heart leaped. Revathy had just updated her WhatsApp status. No, wait. She was now adding more. The circle got many more lines. 15, 20 and it got adding. Was she getting mad? Dev thought with a smile.

He opened her update with shaking fingers.

They were screen shots of WhatsApp chat messages.

" Thank you gopal sir, for the wish"

" Thank you Veena"

" Thank you Aiswarya"

" Thank you Vineeth sir"

" Thank you Acha"

" Thank you Nalini Aunty"

And the list grew on...

It was her birthday. People were awake and wishing this girl at midnight. So many of them.

And she put up a screen shot as and when she got a wish. Most of them had wished her with her image and a golden crown.

Dev was feeling bit jealous about wishes originating from male contacts. Why? He didn't know.

Should he wish her? Dev was pretty unsure. Will she feel bad? Will she think that I am making a move? Messaging her at this hour? Or will she feel happy? Questions kept piling up.

As was her status updates. It was adding on at a steady pace now.

Dev couldn't resist now. What if he wished. As such so many were doing that. And she is happily displaying every message she is receiving. She won't feel bad, hopefully.

He flipped the gallery, for one of her photos. He found some pretty ones; which he had downloaded from her earlier status updates. He was getting creative now. Dev laughed.

He found this one photo, where she stood smiling on a sea beach, with sunrays lighting up her face. She looked very beautiful in her Meesho special flowered long frock.

He forwarded it to her, with a caption..

" Happy birthday Revathy. God bless you"

As bland as it can get. How the messages cover up true emotions.

He kept holding the chat box. She was online. He waited with his heart beat rising now. Suddenly, his message got blue ticks.

His heart suddenly stopped.

She had seen her message. Oh god. She was typing back. And now her message popped up on his screen.

"Thank you Dev. Means a lot coming from you. I thought you might have forgotten me."

And she was typing again.

"BTB, don't you people sleep? Awake at this time?

She sent few funny smileys.

'Losing sleep over you, Revathy'. He wanted to reply. But he only typed this in.

"No Revathy. Just came in. Happy to know it is your birthday. Enjoy your day"

" Thank you Dev".

Dev wished he could continue. He didn't know how. He simply cut off her chat box, with a longing feeling.

He now checked her status.

There surely it was. Screen shot of his wish.

" Thank you Dev"

TWENTY

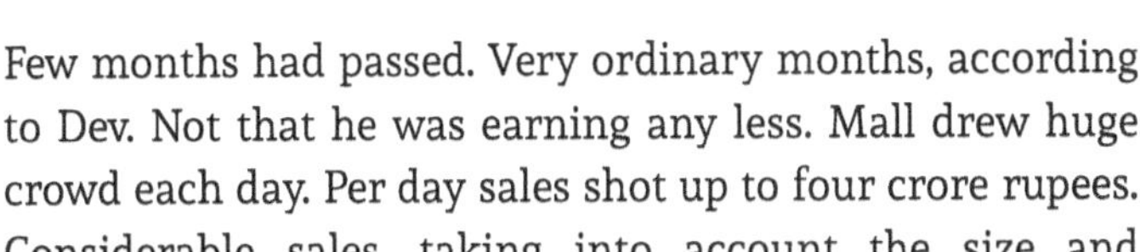

Few months had passed. Very ordinary months, according to Dev. Not that he was earning any less. Mall drew huge crowd each day. Per day sales shot up to four crore rupees. Considerable sales, taking into account the size and demography of Palakkad.

His villas were selling too. And the Emerald Project at Kallekkad was coming up beautifully. They were nearing completion of structure levels. Many had been sold. Some were in negotiation and paper work stages.

Still, for Dev, the months were ordinary.

There were no messages between him and Revathy. As always, he hesitated to take the lead.

"What if she feels bad?" He thought.

He had this temptation of commenting on her status updates many a times. But, again, he felt shy. It is bad to be good sometimes. He thought, with a funny smile.

"If you don't want to comment on her status, don't do. Why don't you try putting a status yourself Dev brother? And see if she comments. Brother, men have to take lead. Don't expect girls to do that"

His cousin and his soul keeper, Siddarth told him one day. Siddarth stayed in Chittur , around fifteen kilometers from Dev. He was running a super market in Chittur. Sometimes Dev used to visit his store. He trusted Siddu. And siddu loved his elder brother. Dev had told him about this girl. He had to confide this with someone. And no one better than Siddu.

"There is nothing, still, I feel, I like her".

He had told him once. Since then Siddu was curious how the thing is progressing.

"Try putting some status update, Dev brother. For example, you can post your mall ads, your villa project ads, or some psych quotes. See if she comments. If she comments, she is ok for a conversation. Do that Dev brother. Or else, find her home, go straight and ask her parents. Who will deny Mr. Devanarayan?"

"Ok Siddu. I will do. But, I will block you from seeing my updates. Don't want you to see how badly am doing."

Dev laughed.

Siddu laughed too. "Do any damn thing, but try something to catch her attention."

That night, Dev put a status update for first time in his life.

" The Emerald Mall..life is calling"

It had an impressive image of the mall with its tag line.

Nothing happened for two hours after he put it up. Some of his friends had sent a thumps up icon or a very nice icon. He ignored them with impatience.

He had a quick dinner that day. Sarada was not at all happy with what he ate. Before his father could catch him for some daddy talk, he sneaked into his bedroom.

Phone was on his bed. He picked it up to see if there were any fresh messages.

Some of his classmates, his advocates, some real estate agents, and his friend Joy, the sitting MLA. All came up with a thumps up.

But nothing from her. He took her chat box. No, she was not online too.

Where are you Revathy?

But, why the poor girl should care. He was the one who was knitting up some weird dreams. She was in her own beautiful world. Bank, friends, and family. Happy and laughing. Poor thing may not even know that someone is waiting for her 'hi'. His mistake. He never let her know.

Night ticked by. No magical words.

He slept off, holding his mobile, spread on his bed, very late that night.

It was nine in the morning, by the time he got up. Probably he slept too late at night. When did he fall asleep? He couldn't fix a time.

He took his phone, and looked at mobile screen. His eyes resisted back the intensive light by trying to close eye lids. Slowly, they got used to the light and opened up.

A long list of unread messages. He started scrolling downwards.

His eyes opened wide now.

There, she was. Her profile picture standing out from the rest.

He opened her message. Sent at 2.30 A.M.

"Hi Dev, it is really a huge mall. I have never been there. Many of my friends went there.

And first time, am seeing your status."

long array of LOL icons.

"Way to go Dev"

And more smileys.

Dev started typing in, as if in a dizzy.

"Good morning Revathy. Thank you so much. Please do visit. Come any time. And let me know before you come. I will be there to take you around. "

"And you messaged me at 2.30. Don't you sleep? "

Dev had a chance to give back what he got the other day.

"And have a nice day"

And he sent few smileys.

May be this was how the people of his age conversed. He was new to unofficial chats.

Dev was now getting more articulate in messages. Or he was at least trying hard.

He got up. When he came back from shower, toweling his head, his screen was on. With a notification of just received message.

It was Revathy. He felt like a champion batter who had just scored a six over the stands, out of the stadium.

Smiling, he opened her message.

"Thank you Dev. It will be a privilege to walk the Mall with the boss. I need not carry my Credit card."

Some innovative laughing icons.

"Will call you and come one day, sure."

"We have an audit going on in our CPC Dev. Hectic it is. Got back really late from bank. Didn't know when I slept off. It was only when I got up early in the morning, I saw your status. So I thought of messaging."

"And I am getting late for office. Bye for now. I will catch you once when I reach office."

And more smileys.

Dev didn't know how to dance. Or he would have broke into one. He just stood there, happy and smiling.

Then, he dialed Siddu. He came on line at the first ring.

"Hello"

"Champ, it worked. She messaged me."

Dev's happiness was ringing in his voice. Siddu laughed happily.

Finally. He thought.

"Now at least, don't hesitate brother. She is okay to chat with you. Keep sending your heart. She won't feel bad. Carry on brother."

Dev went down. Sarada was ready with breakfast. He smiled at her. He had a heavy breakfast that day. He was feeling very hungry. Sarada stood near him, rubbing his hair, happily.

TWENTY-ONE

Vasu was glad to see Dev very happy that day. Dev seemed to be his old assuring self once again.

That day Baby was not with them. Electrification works of Kallekkad project had started, and so he was at site to oversee works.

First, they went to the mall. Vasu followed Dev to his office, carrying some files. General Manager of the mall was waiting for him.

Dev had lifted this guy from a mall in kochi. A very experienced man.

Dhananjayan. Aged fifty four. He took considerable weight off the shoulders of Dev.

They had deep discussions for around one hour. Vasu, waited in the lounge. He knew when not to interfere. Though Dev would never mind, he kept himself out of official meetings. He didn't want to hurt the egos of high ranking managers.

But it was only natural that Vasu got preferential treatment from them. Anything to be taken up with Dev, first they took up with Vasu. He was a kind of bridge.

"Don't come now. Boss is bit dull. Not in proper temper." He would say some day.

"If you guys need anything to be sanctioned, come at once. Boss is in tremendous mood. We are starting from home."

He had texted the GM, before starting from home.

Vasu was their short cut. And he was always a sport. Protecting Dev from unnecessary tensions when he was not feeling ok, or helping with right ground level information whenever Dev wanted.

GM gone, Dev, quickly reached for phone.

" Hi Dev. Reached office. I feel happy that you are texting me. The very own Devanarayan. Where are you? Had food?"

Smileys, in various forms

"Right now, in Mall. Yeah. I had. When are you coming here?"

"Very soon, Dev. I really wish to come. This Saturday? It is fourth Saturday. Off for me."

Smileys.

Dev was now feeling lot comfortable in communicating with her.

" Why not now?"

He texted back.

A bunch of decent smileys followed.

It seemed to say, boss, I know what you mean.

"Let me earn my bread Mr. Capitalist. I will come on Saturday. Definitely. Would wish to see what the boss does in a Mall."

Dev smiled back in smileys. Though he was impatient he texted OK.

She went off line.

Today is Wednesday. Two more days to go. It felt like two years to Dev. How to pass two days? Without being aware of the minutes passing by? Without looking at the clock every thirty seconds?

He had only one answer.

"Vasu, let us go to Tirupur. Let us take Mom and dad too. We are coming back on Friday. "

Vasu didn't understand this sudden decision of Dev. It was true that they had not been to Tirupur factory for past two months. Dev seemed not in a mood to go anywhere. Last month Keerthana and Sitaraman sir had come down from factory, for getting files signed by Dev. And when they were done, Vasu had taken both to the Mall. Dev had given him instructions to take them. First time in Palakkad, first time in his Mall. They were his guests.

By afternoon Sarada, Sundaram, and Dev started to Tirupur, with Vasu at the wheels. They had not stayed in Tirupur, after they shifted to Palakkad. They were all happy. Particularly, Sarada. She had lot to catch up with. She was returning there after a gap of three years.

Dev had made a guest house on top floor of the factory building. Though small, it was comfortable. Dev used to stay there, when he needed to stay at factory for the night. Sarada and Sundaram were staying there for the first time.

People at company were happy to see their boss and family. Dev's cousins came running. It was an unannounced visit. Still, Dev was happy to find everything going well. Keerthana and Sitaraman sir came down from office. Sarada and Sundaram talked to all, enquiring about their families and health.

" Where is Karthi?"

Sundaram asked.

" He left us. " Dev answered with a resigning tone. He had not told Sundaram about Karthi. Sitaraman and Keerthana exchanged looks.

Evening, they went to Venkat's home. The house they had lived in, for years. Sundaram and Sarada were overcome with emotions when they saw Venkat's mother.

Jyothi akka, Venkat's sister, too was there. She had come on a visit from her in-laws house at Semmedu.

Dev remembered visiting her home with Venkat Annan. It was a beautiful place. Acres of sugarcane fields around their house. Jyothi Akka's husband Natarajan was a farmer. They had a makeshift factory where they extracted raw jaggery from sugarcane. As a kid, he had enjoyed those two days stay at Jyothi's place.

Venkat came at around seven in the evening. He was happy to see all. He shook hands with Vasu.

" He grew up here". He told Vasu proudly, pointing at Dev.

Dev's black BMW was parked in front of the house.

" Big car, Dev. How much did it cost? Ten lakhs?"

Dev laughed.

"It is BMW venkat Anna, it cost above one crore"

Venkat was shocked to hear it's price tag.

" One crore? Too much Dev. Our families can live for generations with that kind of money."

It was true. Venkat Annan lived a simple life. Still unmarried, he used a cycle to go to his company. Worked there, returned home, watched films on weekends, and took evening walks. It was a simple, satisfied life.

"Care to walk Anna?" Dev asked.

"Anytime Dev, with you."

Leaving Sundaram and Sarada at Venkat's home, Dev, Venkat and Vasu set out for walk.

"Hi Dev, where are you?"

Her message flashed, when they had reached new bus stand. They had ordered their regular plate of Kaalaan and were waiting.

"Walking with my friend." Dev answered.

"Where? Fort Maidan? I too need to walk. Putting on weight"

Smileys.

"No Revathy. Am at Tirupur now"

Dev replied back.

"Tirupur? You big people. When did you go?"

"Came in the afternoon. I will return on friday night. In time, to welcome a princess, on Saturday."

He sent along with beaming smileys.

A smiley, happy face, with three heart shapes, came in reply. She was touched.

"Thank you Dev. You carry on. Bye."

"Bye". Dev finished.

Venkat exchanged looks with Vasu. Vasu nodded, smilingly.

"Who is it Dev?" Venkat asked with a teasing smile.

"Revathy..."

Dev answered after a pause. He was cutting a shy smile.

TWENTY-TWO

Dev returned with family on Friday night.

His heart was bouncing with joy. He had received message from Revathy.

"I am coming on Saturday Dev. Hope you will be there."

Dev had waited for that message, seemingly, all his life. How he passed two days, he alone knew. Tossing on bed all night, he slept badly on both days.

"I will be there Revathy. You will be my guest. What time you are planning to come?"

Another bland message, though he was erupting with happiness inside.

"We bankers are tuned to 10 A.M. will it be convenient to you?"

Even 2 AM was convenient to him. Dev sent another bland message though.

" Nothing important at that time Revathy. No meetings scheduled for tomorrow. 10 AM is perfectly ok for me."

Can't she make it earlier? He wanted to ask her. Why stick to banking hours even tomorrow?

" Thanks Dev. See you at 10 then."

" See you too"

Dev didn't feel like sleeping that night. He switched on TV. Flipped through English Movie channels. Ten minutes later, he tried History and National Geographic channels.

Few minutes later, he switched off the TV.

What next?

He found few Architectural magazines on tea poy. He flipped through pages for next one hour. The designs and narrations didn't stick in his mind.

It was around 11.30 night. An incoming message notification. It was Revathy.

"Dev, slept?"

How can he. " No" he replied.

"Meeting for the first time. Nervous?"

His heart was thundering inside.

"No Revathy. Why should I? What about you?"

He acted normal.

"A bit. But it is ok. I know I am safe. A girl knows."

Smileys.

He sent few in reply.

"Good night Dev. Be in time."

I will open the Mall myself tomorrow. He joked to himself.

"Good night Revathy".

Morning he called Vasu. "Take leave today. You have worked hard for past few months. Take rest. "

"But sir, I am already on the way."

"Then turn back. You are sacked for today."

Dev laughed.

Vasu turned back, scratching his head. Something wrong with the boss these days. He thought.

"I will have breakfast from Mall mom. I am starting early. Got some work."

He replied to Sarada's questioning looks as he descended stairs to the porch.

By 9.15 he was inside Mall. Security staff saluted with some kind of shock. Too early for the boss.

Cleaning staff were on the job, in all floors. He took a look on all floors and went inside his office. There he sat for next 30 minutes, alone. He didn't want to display his nervousness.

Phone rang at 9.45. Revathy.

The first time she was calling, after they were on messaging terms.

"Hi Dev, am starting from here. Coming on my scooty. Will it be trouble for you, if you come to the parking space? I feel nervous to walk alone into the Mall. "

"I will be there Revathy. Don't worry."

"See you then, I am starting now" she fixed it, with her sweet voice.

Dev walked down from his office. He had not thought about what others may think, if they see their boss walking with a girl. Certainly he would draw questionable looks.

Hell with the world. He thought. Let me not suck up this day.

He reached parking space for two wheelers and waited.

Few people who passed him, and few staff, who recognised him, wished him. Dev was getting nervous now. He raised his hand in a wish every time he got one.

He wished Revathy would come soon.

A pink colour scooty was now visible at a distance. It was coming to the parking space. Slowly, the figure of the girl got visible.

She was wearing a black floral long frock. The smiling lips under the visor, announced Revathy.

Dev was going weak now.

She came near and parked her scooty. She had removed her helmet, by the time Dev reached near her, walking. She got down from her scooty and smiled at him.

God.

Dev missed few heart beats. She was so beautiful.

She walked towards him, gracefully. Swaying beautifully to both sides, with delicate foot placements. Beaming at him. Hair flowing around her shoulders in layers. A slight wind unsettling them, and she pulling it back, with a nice movement of hand.

"Hi Dev"

She reached near him. She smelt of roses.

Her skin complexion. She appeared to be made of 50 kilograms of butter.

Dev even felt she may melt away in sun light now.

"Revathy, I am happy that you came."

And they started walking towards the Mall entrance.

"Nice shirt. You are looking handsome"

Dev was wearing a black casual shirt and a light blue jeans.

Dev smiled at her. His nervousness was now slowly getting better.

"Thanks Revathy. You look beautiful too. You have any Punjabi connection?"

Revathy laughed. "No Dev, am a proper mallu."

Others were looking at them now.

They walked silently for some time. They got into the floor.

Dev could feel her warmth, even when she walked at a comfortable distance.

She was walking with the exuberance of a child, looking in all directions, eyes wide open.

"This is huge and grand Dev. I can't believe it's boss is walking by my side now".

Dev just smiled.

It was he, who couldn't believe, she was walking by his side.

"Where do you live Revathy?"

"And parents?"

"Presently we are put up at Hitech Avenue. Flat 12 A. Easy for me to commute to office and back. And only mom Dev. Father expired long back. He was from the Army."

Then the defence connection accounted for her looks, if not Punjabi. Dev made a hopeless guess.

"Hitech Avenue? So we live very close by. Along border of this highway"

Dev smiled at her.

"I live inside this campus. I will show you my home, when we get to the top floor".

She smiled. In the mood lightings of the Mall, she looked even more beautiful.

"Want to purchase something?"

Dev asked.

"One of the wisdom which my mom gave me is that you never shop with a man. He will never have that patience. He gets you hurry with your decisions and you end up with a wrong shade or size that doesn't fit you well"

She laughed.

Dev took that insult just for the way she laughed.

They were walking. They had reached the food court.

"Can I buy you something? Size and shade doesn't apply here." Dev asked.

She laughed again. They went in.

She ordered some fancy snack, which Dev doubted, it existed. He ordered a coffee.

Dev was wrong. The cafe boy brought what Revathy had ordered. It looked like a fancy sandwich to Dev. With many colourful layers. He felt proud of his food court.

"Nice food Dev. And ambience too. You designed it all yourself?"

"Thanks Revathy. It is impossible to design everything yourself. We leave it to the best architects. "

He was wondering now who had designed her. Such perfect eyes and eyelashes; that made his Mall look horrible.

They walked out again.

They had reached his office entrance. She looked at his name board.

"Impressive. Won't you invite me in?"

Dev hesitated.

"Nobody is in there Revathy".

"Don't worry. You will be safe."

She giggled.

He opened the door for her.

She walked in, taking in the ambience of the huge office. It even had a mini golf court, a game Dev was recently learning.

" Our chairman's office will look pale in front of this Dev. You big people live like kings"

Dev remembered those slaps. And Sukanya. Two things that made him reach here.

"A selfie, Dev? For loving memory of this day with you?"

"Ok" Dev stammered.

She came to stand by his right. She was dangerously close to him now. His heart beats fluctuated badly.

She lifted her right hand for that selfie shot. Revathy smiled widely, at an unbelievable angle. Dev smiled too.

Click.

"Thanks Dev. It has been a wonderful day."

Dev was finding it difficult to talk, with overwhelming emotions.

They walked to the parking space and to her scooty. It was past lunch time.

It was a nice feeling. She walking by his side. How beautifully she walked.

"Won't forget this day. See you again Dev"

"Bye Revathy" Dev said involuntarily.

She flew out in her scooty.

Dev stood, as if some organs have been plucked out through his mouth.

What a day. What an amazing girl.

Dev could not stop smiling, whole day.

TWENTY-THREE

Second wave of Covid had hit Kerala. And it started spiking up.

Once again restrictions were in place. Lock down on Sundays, limitations in shopping hours, restrictions for travelling in a group or gathering in a group etc.

It was the restrictions in banking hours that interested Dev the most. As such he followed banking Calendar these days. He kept himself free from any schedules on banking holidays.

Before giving out any appointments he would look at calendar. He was now conscious of the banking holidays. He would request them to reschedule, if anything came on banking holidays.

He wanted to be free on those days.

Banks were working on alternate days during second wave. That too, with fifty percent of original strength. Which meant Revathy worked only once in five or six days.

She was free for most of the days. That made Dev happy. They had ample time to talk to each other.

One day Revathy had posted a status video. She had captioned it " For your eyes only Prince" with a smiley.

It was a zumba dance. She was rocking in sports attire and dancing superbly. She had great structure, Dev noted with a bit of guilty feeling.

"You dance very gracefully Revathy."

He omitted the comment on her structure wisely.

"Thanks Dev. Do you do any work out?"

Dev was of ideal weight. And he didn't have much time for workouts usually. He sometimes took long walks inside his campus. His only workout.

"No Revathy. Usually no time. I walk in the evenings, when I finish with works early."

"Get up early in the morning, and do some zumba. It will make you light Dev. Try it."

"I dance badly Revathy."

"Who cares? Just follow my video. Throw your hands here and there. Burn calories."

Smileys, again.

"Happy just to see you dance. Won't mock that dance form. Don't you walk?"

"Not possible to walk alone, early in the mornings. Girls have this problem. You guys stare a lot."

"The problem is you get uncomfortable, when you are stared at so much."

LOL smiley.

Dev smiled in return.

After a pause she typed again.

"But, if you come, I can walk with you. Can you come at 5? Will you get up?"

"I won't sleep."

Dev replied. Now he was comfortable saying anything to her.

Plenty of LOL icons came in reply.

"Tomorrow, then?"

"Why not today?"

Dev asked with a prank icon.

"For today, have your lunch, prince. Come tomorrow at 5 AM. I will wait near Manapullikkavu temple road. "

"Done".

Dev sent a bunch of smileys.

It was still dark , when Dev started his Fortuner. That was his favourite car for short trips.

Lights shined brightly along the highway. Few early risers were already walking on the side of the road. Some wore shining arm bands. Experience. A group of cyclists with proper rigs, passed opposite to him.

So much happening at this hour. Dev wondered. He was first time out at this hour, after many years.

He parked his car near the road turning towards Manapullikkavu. He got down and went and stood near the junction.

4.59.

When did he become so punctual? He wondered, with a smile.

Sharp 5 , Revathy came in her scooty.

"Dev, did you sleep?"

She asked, when they started walking to the right side of the road, towards Fort Maidan.

"I won't lie. Slept badly. Kept looking at clock."

He replied with a shy smile.

She looked gorgeous in her sports rig. Dev tried hard not to look at anywhere except face.

"You look beautiful Revathy."

He commented when he couldn't control himself.

"Thanks Dev."

She got shy now. She dropped her eyes.

They walked in silence for some time. Dev was aware of her lovely presence, walking alongside him, almost floating on the road.

"Where did you graduate Dev?"

She asked.

Dev was silent for some time.

"I discontinued after +2 Revathy. I am uneducated, compared to you. "

Revathy looked at him now. Their eyes met. He saw questions in her eyes.

"You see me now Revathy; Successful and somewhat rich. My past is not that colourful."

"Would like to hear about it"

Revathy said earnestly.

"Long story, princess. Some other day."

He smiled.

"What about you?"

She was walking silently.

"My story is simple Dev. Born to Army father. Mother was a teacher there in Army school. We stayed in many places, as father got transfers frequently. Now presently in Palakkad, after I got job. "

"But now I am more interested to hear your story."

She was eyeing him through the corner of her eyes. May be she was shy too. She was smiling looking down.

"Very soon you will know the story. I promise." He smiled.

They walked, the balance distance, looking at each other and smiling. Dev felt like walking on clouds.

It was six, by the time they went their own ways. Dev was feeling very happy. His feelings for her were now getting very intense.

That night, he took up his phone, and jotted down few lines, in Malayalam. His mother tongue. He remembered he used to write poems as a kid. He smiled at the final product.

TWENTY-FOUR

"I love Revathy. She is cute. And bold too...Really like that girl "

Gayathri was happy, as Revathy was getting some attention now.

I smiled in return.

"I remember our college days. When you used to come behind me like a shadow"

She eyed me, with a shy smile and went back to watching a show in TV.

I smiled and returned to the laptop.

I was also getting very much interested in them now.

TWENTY-FIVE

Restrictions on banking hours went on for two months. Which meant, Revathy was free for most of the time.

One day she posted a video of her doing classical dance . Dev didn't know she had learnt classical dance.

"You dance very gracefully. Especially the movement of your eyes. Have you learnt Bharathanatyam?"

" Thank you Dev. I did my 'arangetram' at sixteen. "

Smileys with three hearts.

"You are making me feel hopeless, Revathy. How much is left for me to know about you"

"Keep searching tycoon. You will keep finding me."

Smileys.

He wanted to say his heart out. But, as always, held back.

Few days later she posted her oil painting. A girl, lost in night, looking at the moon.

"This too? That too oil on canvas. You keep amazing me Revathy. Where do I stand compared to you?"

"Dev, you have achieved what others take decades to achieve. I am just doing an oil painting. BTB, my painting is coming up in Palakkad district online painting exhibition, scheduled in two days."

She promptly forwarded a brochure explaining the details of the upcoming exhibition. There, among few other painters, she was portrayed.

"All the best Revathy."

"Thank you Dev. You know, tomorrow we have a training at Thrissur. Pearl Residency. So I will be tied up tomorrow. Don't feel bad."

Dev's heart fell.

"What time do you finish?"

"Training is up to 5 PM."

"Ok Revathy. Then, I will catch you after that. You don't worry."

Dev had made his plans.

Next day, he boarded Kerala State transport bus to Thrissur. He sent Vasu away with the car to Tirupur, to get some files. Vasu would have never let him to travel in a bus.

He was travelling in a bus after many years. He enjoyed the ride. The wind on the face, the stops, the different people who boarded and got down.

He had worn a sunglass, and a mask, to avoid recognition. He didn't want to answer too many questions. Not today at least.

He reached Thrissur bus stand at 5.10 PM. It must have been ten minutes, since Revathy finished with her training.

He dialed her number. As always a prompt hello came from the other side.

"Where are you princess? Finished class?"

"Just finished Dev. Catching an auto to bus stand now. No messages today no?. Missed?"

"I start missing you the next second you stop talking to me. "

Dev answered, sending her few smileys.

"Where are you now Dev? Office? Or walking without me?"

"Am here princess. In Thrissur bus stand. Waiting for a beautiful girl."

He laughed.

" What? "

Revathy squealed in surprise.

"You are here? You no, you are crazy. Wait, I am coming."

She reached in an auto, in another five minutes. She was wearing a dark blue sari with contrasting reddish blouse. She had made up her hair in a traditional way and wore Jasmine flowers. She was looking more beautiful in sari.

"Close your mouth Dev. Something may go inside"

She giggled.

"Where is your car?"

"I came by bus."

She opened her mouth now.

"Bus? Dev, you are doing too much for me."

Her eyes got wet now.

"I wished to travel by your side Revathy. For a change."

They got in the bus and sat in a two seater. She sat by the window and he sat near her.

He could feel warmth of her body against his shoulders.

They enjoyed the travel. Winds flowing in, crowd pressing them against each other. and the wonderful feeling of each other's company.

It was Dev's was first time travel to Thrissur. Revathy kept explaining him the stops on the way. She was very talkative. She could talk hours even on the dumbest subjects.

She laughed, talked, corrected her hair, corrected the position of her palloo, and again talked.

Bus must have reached a spot around two kilometers from bus stand. They heard an explosive sound now.

Everyone got scared and looked at each other, searching for clue what happened.

Conductor of the bus got down. A minute later, he came up shaking his head.

"Tyre burst. Bus won't move now. All of you can get down. I will board you all in the next bus to stand."

And they all got down and stood crowded around the conductor, waiting for the next state transport bus.

"It is just one kilometer to your flat Revathy. Shall we walk?"

She was always a sport.

"Ofcourse. With you, whatever. She smiled at him, looking into his eyes.

Dev felt shy again. They started walking.

It was getting dark. And they walked on the side of the highway, keeping far clear of the vehicles on highway.

It was nice time to walk. Small wind blew on their faces.

They walked happily, talking and looking at each other, for next 40 minutes.

"Tomorrow, after inauguration of online painting exhibition, meet me Dev. Day after tomorrow, am going to mom's place. At Mudappallur. Won't be there for one week. So do meet ok?"

"One week?" Dev expressed his shock.

"Yes Dev. Got to go. Some function at mom's family. So don't miss out tomorrow. "

She pleaded, smiling at him.

"Ofcourse Revathy. Soon after inauguration of your exhibition. Dial when you finish with it."

And Dev dropped Revathy at the entrance of her flat.

"Good night Dev."

She waved her hand beautifully while walking towards the elevator.

"Good night."

Dev kept waving his hand, till the doors of the lift closed after her.

TWENTY-SIX

The Mall was starting to pick up crowd, as Dev and Revathy sneaked out of its parking lot in Dev' s fortuner.

She had come in her scooty at 10 AM.

"You never get out of your banker skin? Right? "

Dev asked jokingly about her timing.

"Once a banker, always a banker."

She laughed.

"Where do we go now?"

Dev asked.

"I have full day. Take me where ever your heart says. "

"And..." she drew on

"...Do tell me your story. I am waiting to hear it for past few months."

Dev turned his car towards Coimbatore.

"Have you been to Isha Yoga center?"

"I have heard about it. But no."

"We are going there. You should see that place. Worth going 70 odd kilometers"

"Anything you suggest Dev. Am with you."

The Isha Yoga Center, situated at the foothills of Velliangiri, on the outskirts of Coimbatore, is the headquarters for Isha Foundation.

Isha Foundation is a nonprofit, spiritual organization, founded in 1992, near Coimbatore, India, by Jaggi Vasudev, or Sadhguru. It hosts the Isha Yoga Centre, which offers yoga programs under the name Isha Yoga. The foundation is run "almost entirely" by volunteers.

The center offers all four major paths of yoga – kriya (energy), gnana (knowledge), karma (action), and bhakti (devotion), drawing people from all over the world.

It has Dhyanalinga, The Linga Bhairavi temple, The Theerth khund, Surya Khund and the recently added 112 foot tall Adiyogi and Aadiyogi aalayam as the main attractions.

People throng from all over the world to see this place.

Dev chose that place, as he had been there once. He liked the peaceful ambience there. He was impressed not only by Sadhuguru's vision, but also his architectural skills, in building that beautiful place. And in so less time. And that tasty lunch and other savouries in the canteen. Everything prepared with home grown vegetables and rice.

He told her the history of the place. Revathy was impressed.

"Thanks Dev, for taking me there."

"Now, let me hear about my own Sadhguru."

She said, beaming at him. Dev struggled to meet her eyes.

So much energy in her eyes. They radiate like two miniature suns. Dev thought.

By the time Dev finished his story, they had reached Isha center. Revathy was listening earnestly. With tears in her eyes.

"Inspiring Dev. Your story. You came up all the way from ground zero. You are such a good person."

She wiped her eyes while getting down from his car. She was wearing a red top and blue jeans. Her hair was tied into a pony, and it danced beautifully behind her, as she walked smartly towards Adiyogi, the 112 foot idol.

It was an impressing scene. Both the magnificent statue, with its impressive emotion and the girl walking towards it now.

Dev followed her with a smile.

She ran around the idol like a little kid and kept taking selfies with him. And they walked towards the Dhyanalinga entrance, with the maize fields to their left. It was a beautiful setting. With the Velliangiri hills in backdrop, the relishing Adiyogi behind, beautiful maize fields spanning out on their left, and the impressive Dhyanalinga in their front.

Lots of naagas in its architecture. And beautifully used.

It was pin drop silence inside. Truly, a welcome silence. People just hung around the place for the peace it offered.

They skipped the dip at Theerth Khund. They went inside Dhyanalinga, and sat in meditation. Revathy had never experienced the power of meditation or positive energy. Through half open eyes she now looked at Dev. By that time her eyes had got used to the darkness inside.

Dev was staring at her. With folded hands to the front and face turned to his left, where she sat.

She felt shy for the first time. She closed her eyes.

Now, they walked around, really close. They were now ok with an occasional brushing of their shoulders.

They had their lunch at Isha Canteen. A fabulous vegetarian lunch.

Rice, sambar, Rasam and all those ubiquitous items that made a South Indian Thali.

"Dev, it is really tasty."

she curved her left hand fingers together to indicate its superior taste.

"All made with home grown veggies and rice, Revathy."

Dev smiled. He was happy that she was enjoying.

It was 7 PM, by the time they got to the Mall parking.

Both sat in silence for some time, after the car had been parked near her scooty.

"Thanks Dev." Her eyes were moist again.

And with a sudden motion, she opened the door of the car to get down. May be she wished to hide her tears.

"Bye Dev."

She got down from the car and walked to her scooty.

Swaying beautifully.

It would be days, before Dev could see her again. Dev sat, broken, at that damn thought, holding the steering wheel.

Any time, before she reaches her scooty, he could still get down the car, stop her, for another couple of minutes with her.

But, something held him back tight in his seat.

The days without her...

The thought almost choked him to death.

Revathy, now positioned herself on her scooty and turned to face him. She smiled one last time, hiding her tears, and whizzed past.

Dev sat there, burning inside, unable to move.

TWENTY-SEVEN

Revathy went to her native place the next day.

Dev now knew, how important she has become for him. Without her, he felt as if he got trapped in a black hole. Time, place and distance didn't matter anymore. It was all the same. Whether it was 7 AM in the morning or 11 PM at night. Whether it was his comfortable bedroom, or the construction site wilting in scorching heat. He didn't feel any difference. She had left a vacuum around him.

"Hi Dev, I reached. Will message you when I get time. Too many people roaming around me. Don't want to raise eye brows. You take care please."

She messaged the next minute she reached her native home.

Then it was silence.

Days went by. Most of the time, Dev remained in his office at the Mall or the Kallekkad construction site. Being with Vasu or Baby was a bit of comfort for him. It diverted his thoughts. Even though Revathy played in the background of his mind.

Three days before her scheduled arrival, Revathy messaged him at night.

"I am coming tomorrow Dev."

Dev sent few very happy icons.

"Welcome princess. I am lost without you."

"Don't be so happy Dev."

Few LOL icons followed.

"Tomorrow night, I have to catch a flight to Hyderabad. From Coimbatore. Two days training at State Bank training center. They are recalling me from leave. Will you drop me?"

Red faced icons. The shy ones.

Dev was happy and sad at the same time. Happy that he can travel with her again. Sad that she will be going again.

"Ofcourse Revathy. I will drop you. I am dying without you. Anything to see you."

"What time?"

"Flight is at 2 AM. Let us go by 9 PM Dev. So that you can return in time. Come straight to my flat. Mom is staying back here in Muduppallur. So I will be free. "

"Ok princess. So nine PM tomorrow."

Dev was exploding with happiness. Tomorrow he will be seeing Revathy again.

She reached the next day at 7 PM. Her maternal uncle dropped her. So Dev didn't have much hope.

"I will be ready by 9 Dev. You come. I will wait near Flat entrance. Dying to see you."

Smileys with three hearts.

"Skip the flight. I will drop you to Hyderabad. I can't imagine that you are going again."

He sent, along with few prank icons.

"Useless to come there Dev. We will be busy like anything for two days. Intensive training. And we need to stay in the campus. Poor Dev will have to wait there again. You are better waiting for me here in Palakkad. At least it will be comforting for me to that you are safe here."

"Be ready Revathy. I am coming at 9."

Dev didn't want to break down. He kept it short.

At sharp 9, his Fortuner entered into the entrance of Hitech Avenue. She was waiting there, with a shoulder bag on, and a trolley bag to her side.

She smiled widely, on seeing Dev's car.

She shone like demi god in half darkness. She seemed to radiate an aura around her.

Dev got down to help her get her luggage on board the car.

"You travel light, for a girl" Dev commented teasingly.

"Brought up in Army camps. We know how to keep it light Dev".

She laughed.

Dev had forgotten that part. They are auto trained to do anything in a special way. The defence veterans and their families.

They started towards Coimbatore airport.

She kept on talking about training. And then got diverted to her paintings when she thought she had finished with her training subject.

She showed him her whatsapp chat with another painter.

She had sent him the photo of the painting she did the previous day. For seeking his comments on it.

And he had sent a voice message.

"See, he is such a good painter. Lucky that I am getting his guidance."

She started showing Dev some of the paintings of the senior painter.

Mohana Krishnan.

Dev observed his name from the chat box.

He felt jealous. And he burnt uncontrollably inside. His heart suddenly fell. He was getting that feeling for first time. It was unbearable.

Revathy kept on talking for some more time, till she finally observed that Dev was not responding. He had fallen silent.

She looked at him. His face had shrunk and had lost its colour.

She looked at the open chat box, in her mobile.

She suddenly became aware of the meaning of Dev's silence.

She smiled.

"Dev, he is 63. My dad's age. A retired professor from Arts college. He is mentor for few painters in Palakkad. Please don't feel bad."

She begged in a beautiful voice, looking expectantly at Dev.

63?

Dev felt relieved. To some extent.

He looked at Revathy and smiled.

"I am sorry. I got jealous. Frankly."

"You don't have to be jealous Dev. You are the first person who comes to mind when I wake up every day. And you are the first person, I hung around with. Need not be Dev."

She held his arm.

First touch. A shiver went through Dev. All his anguish, jealousy and doubts vanished in a second.

He felt as if he was touched by a bouquet of flowers.

"I am ok now Revathy. Sorry."

Dev smiled foolishly.

After a second of silence, Revathy got busy again. She was very energetic. She couldn't sit idle for a second.

"What you keep in here?"

She opened car's dash board tray and started picking things out from it. She was keeping her head so low as to have a clear view of the contents of the box.

"Dont fall inside!" Dev joked.

She turned to him and sneered.

"eeee"

She took out Dev's sunglass finally. She tried it on, looked in the vanity mirror to appreciate her looks and turned toward Dev.

She looked hot. In sunglasses. Dev appreciated her in sign language. She laughed and kept back the sunglass.

After finishing with the dash board box, as if unsure of what to do next, she sat comfortably, both legs folded and on the seat. She sat silently for a moment, taking in the comfort of sitting in that position.

Then she turned to Dev.

"You always travel in this box no? Cut out from the world?"

Dev now looked at her with questioning glance. He had just negotiated a sharp turn.

"What do you mean Revathy?" Dev asked with a smile.

"I always find you in one or the other car. Driving in a car, you are mercilessly cut out from the real world Dev. Have you tried driving around on a bullet? Like him?"

She pointed at a rider going in front of them. His fancy helmet, jacket, and the flashing lights, provided picture of a professional rider.

Dev shook his head in a no.

"Get out of this moving jail sometimes, Dev. Ride a bullet. Get the wind on your face. Ride a hill. See people passing by. Hear the real sound of world outside. You will have fun."

She said every word with earnestness.

Dev sat thinking about her words.

He dropped her at Airport, in time for the check in. In fact, she ran inside with her luggage, to be in time for the check in. She ran, looking backwards at him, waving continuously. And with a final smile she turned the corner and went out of Dev's vision.

It was 11.30, by the time Dev started back to Palakkad.

Roads were almost empty. Except few passing trucks. And some odd cars. He drove at a steady pace, thinking about Revathy.

He called Vasu. Vasu got up from his sleep with a start.

Boss calling at this hour! Some emergency??

"Hello" he answered the call with some apprehension.

"Vasu, sorry to knock you up at this time. Do me a favour."

"No problem boss. Please tell me."

"I want a bullet, Royal Enfield, the latest version. Book one tonight. I don't bother what you do. I want delivery in two days."

"Boss? Waiting period for Enfield bullet is 6 months."

He expressed his shock at this strange order and at this odd hour.

"That is why I called you. I want it day after tomorrow."

Dev disconnected phone. Vasu scratched his head.

Dev drove in silence then. Till he spotted a BMW car parked on the side of the Highway, near the Nandi statue. Two people were standing on the road, asking for lift.

He stopped his car near to them. He had recognised one of them.

Bharath. The celebrated writer. He lowered his left window pane, to talk to him.

TWENTY-EIGHT

Revathy returned two days later. Her mom had not returned from Mudappallur. Her maternal uncle, again played spoil sport. He picked up Revathy from airport.

"Hi Dev. I reached home. I wished you would have come to Hyderabad. Badly missed my prince."

Heart signs.

"Tomorrow is holiday. Meet me Revathy. A surprise awaits you."

"Oho. The man who can never surprise, coming up with a surprise. You are growing up Dev."

She laughed.

"I will definitely come. I too want to meet you, Dev. 10 AM then. "

She sent few heart and prank icons. Those prank icons were meant for the timing.

Her timing always amused Dev. Bankers. He smiled to himself.

She came in at sharp 10. Dev was again waiting at parking space of the Emerald Mall.

She got down her scooty and came towards Dev, flowing in a peach coloured frock. She looked stunning.

She was smiling, and she almost sprinted to him the last few meters.

"I am getting impatient when I am not seeing you even for one day Dev. You charmed me some way. I am not myself now."

Dev smiled.

"You charmed me from day one Revathy. I never complained."

She laughed, covering her mouth.

"Where is the surprise?"

She asked, raising her hands beautifully, in a question.

Dev waved his hand towards his left.

Revathy covered her open mouth again, this time to hide her shock.

It was a shining, red, Enfield. Brand new.

"Dev?? You bought this?"

Dev answered yes, by a slight head shake.

"You are wonderful Dev, and a bit crazy too. And, are we going to stare at this beauty whole day or are we going somewhere?"

She laughed, teasing him.

"Get on the beast, Princess, we start thundering now".

Dev started the bullet, and Revathy Got behind him. Both had helmets and wore sunglasses. It was hard to identify them. Exactly what Dev wanted. But Revathy never seemed to care about that. Defence blood.

Revathy sat, at a safe distance from Dev. She had cushioned the gap with her vanity bag. Dev himself, felt comfortable that way.

"Where are we going Dev?"

Revathy shouted in his ears, to make herself audible. The thunder of the bullet, the speed of the bullet and the wind flowing on their faces; everything made talking at low decibels impossible.

"Nelliyampathy. The hills."

Dev shouted back.

"Wow, it will be wonderful" Revathy almost exploded in his ears.

They had passed Pothundy Dam, and started climbing up, when a slight drizzle came down.

They were not prepared for that. No jackets on, both of them.

They absorbed the drizzle. And both started to feel cold, by the time they negotiated the 17 th hair pin bend. They had covered almost three fourth distance to reach the top.

Dev parked the bullet under a large tree, standing below the road.

They stood in the shadow of the thick leaves of the tree. Safe from the drizzle. But they were feeling cold. She was sitting on the bullet and looking at the Pothundy Dam view below. She didn't see Dev staring at her now.

She was bit wet. Rain drops over her hair, her reddish cheeks, lips, and the bare neck. And her beautiful, long hands.

Aware of his stare now, now she turned to look at Dev.

Colour of his eyes had changed. He now directly looked at her eyes. And he went close to her.

She was now sitting opposite to him. Her face inches away from his face.

His breath grew heavier.

She was very close. Dangerously close.

Dev took both her arms in his arms. A shiver went through her body, as he looked longingly at her eyes. Now his lips slowly came down, aiming for her wet lips.

She turned her face away. Unable to control her tears.

"No Dev. I am sorry. I am engaged to someone."

Dev stopped half way in horror, hearing her words.

"Engaged?" He asked, unable to believe her words.

"Yes Dev" she now said, lowering her eyes in guilt.

"Last time when I went to my native place. Ishwar. My distant cousin. He is a software guy, with Face book headquarters."

Dev shook his head in disbelief.

"Why, Revathy? Why now? And why this to me?"

"Every time we met after that, I wanted to tell you Dev. But somehow I didn't want to lose you. I loved each and every second I was with you. Every time I thought I would tell you the next time. And that next time kept postponing. You are too good to lose Dev. I kept holding on to you, as if I was holding on to my life."

Drizzle had stopped.

Dev started the bullet. He didn't say anything.

Revathy got behind him, shaking with emotions now. Her tears flowed uncontrollably. She didn't bother about cushioning the space between her and Dev.

She wished Dev would at least shout at her.

But he didn't say anything. His heart had seemingly stopped beating.

He just wanted to steer this bullet to the Mall. Into the parking space. Where he can safely offload Revathy. To her scooty. So that he can then dash to his home, into the privacy of his bedroom. Where the great Devanarayan, the talk of the State, can just break down, and weep his heart out.

When she got down from bullet, she looked hopefully at Dev. lest he may look at her, lest he may say few words to her.

But he just sped away.

And, weeping hard inside her helmet, she drove towards her flat.

Dev didn't stop to answer the questions of Sarada. He went straight to his bedroom.

He felt shattered.

The great Devanarayan. Young achiever. But where does he stand now? What did he achieve at the end?

He stands lost. Losing his love. Losing his heart.

He fell on his bed. And cried hard, for the first time in life, tears wetting the pillow cover.

His phone was silent till 8.30 PM.

May be Revathy didn't dare to call him up. May be she felt guilty.

Dev kept looking at his phone in half minutes interval.

And it rang at around 9 PM.

Revathy. The name flashed. She finally called.

He wanted to hear her voice now. All evening he was waiting for this call.

He attended the call.

"Dev..." Her voice was unnaturally jittery. It seemed she was struggling for breath.

"Revathy, what happened?" Dev asked almost in a shout.

The change in her voice had made Dev forget about everything that happened in the morning.

"Dev..."She laboriously drew on...

" Dev...come ...save ...me...someone ..." She couldn't complete.

She was breathing hard. And the call got cut.

After a second of shock, Dev dashed down to his car.

On reaching her flat complex, he dashed out, without even caring to switch off the engine.

He ran up all the way to 12 A, without waiting for the lift.

Her door was half open. He entered looking in all directions. Finally, he found her, at the entrance to her bedroom, lying on the floor, in a pool of blood.

Looking at him, with vacant eyes...

Almost lifeless.

He heard footsteps behind, and turned back in hope of getting help.

It was the security. He had followed Dev, seeing his frenzy.

He raised the alarm promptly.

TWENTY-NINE

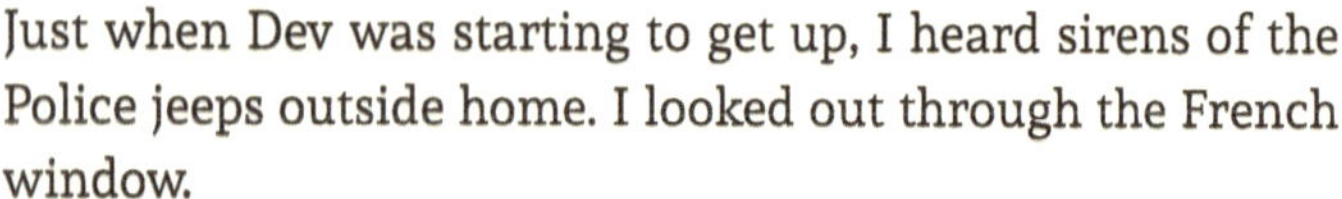

Just when Dev was starting to get up, I heard sirens of the Police jeeps outside home. I looked out through the French window.

Security was opening gates for the police jeeps to come in.

I turned to Dev, with an apprehensive look.

"Dev, police is here"

"Expected that Bharath sir. They may have traced my call to you from Revathy' s flat. I don't care as Revathy is past danger zone now."

He paused and got up from settee.

"But I want you to believe me. I didn't do it."

"I know that Dev"

Calling bell rang for the second time now. With one last look at Dev, I opened the front door.

Police were at the step.

"Sorry to knock you up Bharath sir. I am Inspector Vijay Bhaskar. We came to get Dev sir."

I stood aside. Dev stepped out.

"Sorry Dev sir. We need to follow the available clues. First case after new SP took charge last week. She needs you at District Police Headquarters."

Dev stepped out with him.

I went near the Inspector.

"Inspector Sir, if I can have a word. He didn't do it."

He looked at me, and shrunk his shoulders in a show of helplessness. And smartly turned and walked towards the police jeep.

Dev followed him, silently.

THIRTY

Dev was taken to the District Police Headquarters. They climbed up the stairs to reach SP's office.

Superintendent of Police

The shining brass board on the wall announced the District Police Chief.

He went in with Inspector Vijay Bhaskar.

SP was sitting behind a magnificent table. Dev now looked at the name board on the table.

Sukanya Sakthivel, IPS.

With utter disbelief he looked at the face of the officer, who was studying an open file in front of her.

Dev, looked at her again, with mixed feelings.

His heart erupted in joy.

It was his Sukanya. He won't go wrong here. He has been searching this face in thousands of faces he came across every day.

Aware of their presence now, Sukanya looked up. Her eyes met Dev's eyes. With a faint smile and in official tone she said;

"Dev, please be seated. Inspector, can you wait outside? Need to have a one to one with Dev."

Inspector stepped out smartly, with a salute.

"Sukanya?" Dev asked, utterly taken back now.

"Yes Dev. Took charge last week. I heard you are here. But couldn't meet you, as I was busy with taking over formalities."

"Happy to note you have grown big Dev. Not the young boy I left behind in Tirupur. How is Sarada Aunty and Sundaram Uncle?"

"They are fine Sukanya. I tried your number many times. "

He said, with a guilty tone.

"It changed."

Sukanya said, in a resigning tone.

"I went to Delhi after you left Tirupur. I wanted to take up Civil services seriously. Worked hard for two years. Finally I got IPS."

"I heard about you Dev. All these years. Only that I was pretty tied up most of the time. And sometimes, may be, I hesitated to call you."

Sukanya now looked at him, with beaming eyes. As always, pampering him with her eyes.

"I knew you would spring up some day when I want you the most. Like you did the first time. Thank god you did Sukanya. I want to know who did this to Revathy. We need to find him, Sukanya. Before we lose him"

"We know from the start that it is not you Dev. We just needed to chase up clues. Reavthy got conscious, within one hour of getting admitted in Medical college. She shook her head in denial, when we showed your photo."

"You guys doubted me?" Dev asked in some kind of dismay.

"In an investigation, we need to chase up every loose ends and fit things into propositions. You were with Revathy whole day. And she called you around the time when we suspect the crime to have taken place. You arrived in the scene of crime around that time. We could dig these things out, looking at mobile locations of both you and Revathy. We chased it with the last call Revathy made."

"and you need not worry now Dev. We know it is not you."

"Sukanya, she is an innocent girl. Who may have stabbed that poor girl. Am at my wit's end." Dev broke down.

Sukanya now looked at him with a longing feeling.

"Sad Dev, I had to meet you like this"

After a pause she asked.

"You were in relationship?"

Dev now looked up in guilty feeling. He couldn't meet her eyes.

"I was foolishly addicted to her Sukanya. But she is engaged." And he broke down again.

Sukanya stood up and placed a comforting hand on his shoulders.

"We have a footage, Dev. It is of one of the cameras of the flat where she stayed. We have one suspect cornered out in the footage. He came up the stairs first, and went back in a hurry. And after ten minutes or so, you came."

Dev now looked at her in horror.

He stood up and came close to Sukanya.

"Where is it?"

She showed him the footage on her phone.

And paused it, once the face of the man was almost clear.

Dev recognised him with a shock.

Karthi. His former employee. His former manager at Tirupur factory. He didn't doubt that walk. Quick and stooping forward.

"Sukanya, this is him"

"Karthi. I know Dev. I have seen him on my visits to your factory. Took time to recollect though. Had a feeling I have seen him somewhere. And when I tried to remember the faces connected with you, I suddenly remembered him. Got you here to make sure it is him."

"It is him Sukanya. But why?"

"For that, we need to find him now, Dev."

She rang up some one and shouted to other side, in Tamil.

"Suspect confirmed inspector. It is Karthi. Pick him up."

Dev was now thinking hard.

He remembered Chandran uncle telling him the other day.

"Dev, why is your manager boy roaming around here in Palakkad?"

"Which manager?"

"That fishy one. What was his name? Your manager at Tirupur? I had seen him few times when I came to your factory. Never liked his face."

"Oh, Karthi. He is not in my factory uncle. We sent him off last year."

"But I saw him few times here in Palakkad. He didn't see me though. He still looks fishy. With his foolish cap"

Dev didn't bother at that time. Now everything came back to him in horror.

"Sukanya, I dropped him from company, last year."

Sukanya got alert now.

"Tell me Dev, why was it?"

"He was good. But somehow he started using drugs. He siphoned off large cashes to splurge on drugs. He used to threaten all the employees there, not to tell anything to me. All were scared of him"

He continued after a pause.

"But one girl, Kavitha, from the packing section, spilled it all to me. He made an attempt on her, when she was alone in company. And he was under toxins. The girl somehow escaped with injuries. And she told me everything."

"The next two hours I reached there and sacked him. I didn't file a police complaint then, as his mother came that day and begged me to leave him. He was their only son and hope. I couldn't ignore her tears."

"Oh, it all fits now. Drugs make one insane enough to do anything."

Sukanya remarked.

"Yes. He came back next day. Begging for pardon. I saw syringe punctures all over his hands. His eyes lacked shine. His whole body looked dehydrated. Clear indications of a drug addict"

"But I said no. And he went back silently."

"I understand now Sukanya. He had a vengeance on me. His source of easy funds for drugs dried up after I sacked him. You know that these people will do anything to get money. And can do anything savage in their hours of rage. But why Revathy? That innocent girl?"

Dev broke down again.

"Revenge takes strangest of forms Dev. He wanted to get back at you. He wanted to hit you where it would pain you most. He may have observed you for past one year. And may have cornered out this Revathy."

Dev, now remembered Revathy remarking few times;

"Dev, are we being followed?"

She would look through the back window of the car with concern.

And few occasions Dev had seen a motorbike. But he didn't bother at that time. Too many vehicles on the road, to look at one particular vehicle with suspicion.

"I think you are watching lots of horror movies Revathy" Dev used to tease her.

After few minutes of silence, Sukanya's mobile rang.

"We nabbed him." The other side said.

"From Pollachi. The fellow was trying to sell gold bangles and chain which he took from her. We got there in time. He has admitted to his crime."

"Thank you Inspector. I will send a team." She disconnected the call.

"Dev, Inspector will drop you home. Go home and take rest. Revathy is perfectly all right now. It will take some time to completely heal though. She may need long counseling sessions to get over her anxiety."

"But thank god, she is fine."

Dev smiled in relief.

"Thanks Sukanya. Do come home when you are free. Mom and dad will love to hear that their little girl is now Police chief here."

Sukanya smiled.

"Definitely Dev."

With a thanking smile, Dev stepped out and got in Inspector's jeep.

He dialed Bharath.

"Sir, it was Karthi. He has been caught."

THIRTY-ONE

Revathy looked tired.

Her face lighted up, on seeing Dev. But her efforts at sitting up failed and she resigned to her pillow.

She could just manage a smile at Dev. A very weak smile. Only a shadow of her laughter, smiles and giggles.

Even Dev could return a half smile. A smile, heavy with guilt. In a way, he was the reason. Karthi had chosen to hurt her in order to get back at him. How happy she was, before meeting him. Her status updates. Happy ones. She used to be an easy going girl.

Meeting him got her to this. She lay there, on her bed, covered in bed sheet, face distorted with pain from the abdomen. She had lost lot of blood. That made her very weak.

How much time will it take for her to return to her old self?

Dev, now honestly wished, he had not met her.

Poor girl. Going through physical and emotional pain now. Wound was deep, and it took hours for the doctors to stich it up inside and out.

And the pain she might have been going through emotionally. To break that bitter truth to him, at the last minute.

Though Dev was hurt that time, Revathy's condition made him forget that. He was happy just to see Revathy alive.

He couldn't forget the look on her eyes, when he carried her to the ambulance. He never thought she would make it.

Hell with the emotions and feelings for her. She mattered most. Her life mattered most. Her happiness mattered most.

"Don't bother yourself dear. You need to take complete rest."

Dev said, while taking his seat on a chair near her bed.

Her mother had gone out the moment Dev entered into her room. She was in tears. She wanted to leave them alone.

"Hi Dev. Happy you came. I thought you would never forgive me."

She said weakly, in a sad tone.

He held her hand, fondly.

"Forget that Revathy. I am sorry I behaved rashly that day. To think that, you are going through all this, only because of me. It is making me feel horrible"

"Don't say that Dev. "Her eyes were moist now." This is the minimum I deserve. For everything I did to you."

"But please believe me, Dev" She continued after pausing for catching her breath.

"I was not aware of the engagement part, till I reached home that day. He is son of father's batch mate in Army. Completed his engineering and got placed in FB headquarters. I have heard his name few times."

She continued laboriously now, struggling for breath, her heart clogged with emotions.

"They had come home, asking for my alliance. And mom could not deny. I couldn't blame her, as I hadn't told her about you."

"And I knew, you like me. That hurt me most. I was in a kind of mess. What to do, whom to call, what to talk etc etc"

"You know Dev, I didn't have the energy or will power to go against the tide. Mom was too quick in deciding everything. And she did everything taking me for granted."

"My inexperience, indecisiveness, and inability to assert myself, cost me huge. It was too late to make amends. And I went through the motions."

She wept now. Silently, but heaving with emotions.

"I wanted to tell you all this when I came back from leave. While you were driving me to Airport. But couldn't. Yes Dev. I couldn't. I was looking at you all the time when you were driving. You were so happy to be with me. Taking in each of my words. Laughing at my pathetic jokes. Pampering me with your care. I didn't want to spoil those moments. I postponed the news. With guilt. Crying in my mind."

"And I waited for a moment to tell you this, when we drove to Nelliyampathy. I thought I would tell you, when we reach the top. In at most silence. So that you can shout your heart at me. Burst your emotions on me. I thought I will buy time, for spending those lovely moments with you. Just a little more. But, the rain. It spoiled my timing. And you got hurt. Am sorry Dev. I never meant to hurt you. I never meant to cheat you. "

Dev was silently listening. With nothing but compassion in his heart. He had overcome the first shock. Now, he was ready for the reality.

He looked at Revathy. As if looking at a little kid. They looked at each other for some time. Slowly, Revathy, got over her emotions. Got over her guilt. Her heart beats calmed down. Her nerves started healing.

They smiled at each other. A caring, loving smile.

"Revathy, tell me only this. Did I ever have a place in your heart? I mean, at least, before this guy?"

Revathy, looked at him, without blinking her eyes.

"You need not ask this Dev. You always know. "

Girls never answer anything straight. They always leave something for guessing. Even on their sick beds.

But Dev could easily guess this time. He smiled happily.

"Ishwar talked to you?"

He was now prepared enough to ask her this. Though he didn't sound convincing. Still, Revathy could feel, Dev has now come to terms with the unavoidable truth.

"He keeps calling, Dev. Though he gives me enough time for rest. He is a good guy."

Dev felt at peace with himself now. Calmness prevailed.

Revathy's phone rang. It was on the table near Dev. He took it for handing it over to her.

He could see it was a whatsapp video call. Ishwar's handsome image flashed on the screen.

He didn't feel jealous this time. He gave the phone to Revathy. And stood up to leave. Revathy held his hand.

She looked at him with a mix of various emotions.

Dev, smiled widely at her.

"Talk to him Revathy. You need more of him now. Get well soon."

He left the room in haste. He could hear Revathy's weak voice, talking to Ishwar.

Tears filled his eyes. And he knew he would miss her.

THIRTY-TWO

My third book was launched few months later.

Copies were pre booked in large numbers.

Like last two times, I was getting positive responses.

Gayathri was happy too.

"Where is Dev?"

She asked one day, as I sat monitoring author's dash boards in various online platforms. I felt good on the number of sales.

"He is in Kochi now. He has gone there to meet Revathy. They are going to meet for the first time after the incident. She has joined her new branch at Kochi. After the incident, she was transferred out to Kochi, on doctor's instructions. She needed a change"

"Thank god, she is fine. Such a fine and innocent girl. Are they getting together?"

"Don't think so, Gachu. Such things happen only in stories. She is engaged to an IT professional and they are getting married in few days. Dev is now ok with it. He has finally accepted the fact. He is happy that Revathy is alive. And he needs nothing else"

"Then why is he meeting her now? Won't it cut open the old bruises? Won't it hurt him more?"

"None of that Gachu. Dev has reached a divine stage in love. Where, he accepts that his part has been played out. A suitable match has now come for his love, and he has consented to step

aside. He knows, it is better for her. He knows she will be happy. And he knows, he will be there around her, every time and any time she wants. Whether she will ever want him or not, doesn't bother him now. He just loves her, and will continue doing that. For him she is his journey. Not his destination. "

Gayathri wiped off her tears.

"He is half way in love; and is happy just to continue his journey."

I concluded, with a melancholy tone.

***

Vijay Nair was born on 23rd August 1977 in Tathamangalam, Palakkad, Kerala.

Banker by profession, he is a noted writer, poet and entrepreneur.

He did his schooling from Govt. L. P School, Nallepilly, Govt. UP School, Nalleppilly and Jawahar Navodaya Vidyalaya, Malampuzha. He completed his graduation and MBA, whilst in service in Indian Navy.

From 1996 to 2011, he served in the Indian Navy. Since 2013, he is with SBI and is presently based at Palakkad, Kerala.

Books by Vijay Nair

1. Half way in Love (English Novel)

2. Chila Kallangal Nallathaanu (Malayalam Poetry collection)

3. You are my True North (English Novel)

Wife: Reshmi

Daughter: Amaya

Address:

Amaya, Olive Gardens, Cherad, Malampuzha - 678651